A Sense of Depravity

Melissa Anne Walker

PublishAmerica
Baltimore

© 2006 by Melissa Anne Walker.
All rights reserved. No part of this book may be reproduced, stored in a retrieval system or transmitted in any form or by any means without the prior written permission of the publishers, except by a reviewer who may quote brief passages in a review to be printed in a newspaper, magazine or journal.

All characters appearing in this work are fictitious. Any resemblance to real persons, living or dead, is purely coincidental.

First printing

ISBN: 1-4241-0928-0
PUBLISHED BY PUBLISHAMERICA, LLLP
www.publishamerica.com
Baltimore

Printed in the United States of America

To my brother, Brian, who doesn't like to read but read the whole thing from start to finish. I love you with all of my heart.

I'd like to thank Dr. John and Juliet Emerson for saving my butt twice this summer. Their saving grace has made this manuscript possible. Thanks to everyone who listened to me whine and complain when Sherman ate my only copy and I had to quickly remedy the situation in less then two weeks' time.

1

I heard the music long before I saw the cabin. The only other noises occupying the air were those made by the small creatures that resided in the surrounding woods and, in all actuality, they were not loud enough to drown out the song. It was a familiar song, one I knew from long ago. I followed the music and that's when I discovered the cabin.

Wandering around, cold and hungry I had slept little and worried more. I'd dined on tree bark, berries, grub and small lizards I had managed to trap. I'd pop the little bastards into my mouth and pretend I was eating nice crunchy popcorn…the mental pictures really didn't help but I loathed the taste of meat. I had no choice though as the lizards were in abundance and I was not. It was a simple log cabin set deep in the woods, off the beaten path and away from intruding snoops. Fortunately for me, it was exactly where I needed it to be. It was my log beacon and the person who lived there was to be my savior. I took a deep breath and made my way to the cabin's clearing. The ground around the structure was clean. A metal trash receptacle had been placed approximately 30 feet from the cabin and small wisps of smoke were circling around it. As I was surveying my surroundings the front door of the cabin opened and out bolted a very large black dog and a girl who looked to be my age. The dog noticed me right off and came lunging across the clearing at me. It appeared friendly enough. It wasn't barking and its long tongue was lolling out of its mouth. Its tail wagged in time to a non-existent metronome. I couldn't decide what to do. I thought of dropping to the ground in hopes the dog would lose interest and dart off in the other direction, but that didn't seem to be a working solution. I stepped forward and prepared a quick introductory speech in my head and was just about to open my mouth and speak when the dog hit me full in the chest. I was knocked backward and the air was ripped from my lungs. I was reminded of a *Flintstones* cartoon. Dino the pet dinosaur always greeted Fred in this manner and now I knew, without a doubt, how Fred had always felt. I tried to get the dog off, but his tongue would not quit licking me. Every time I opened my mouth to holler for help, his tongue would squirm its way in, so I opted for silence. I was hoping the girl had been witness to her dog's antics and would soon be there to rescue me. My thoughts flowed to the past few weeks of my own personal hell. I was really praying to my god, Murphy, I wouldn't have to encounter any more dogs for a while. I had been traveling by train prior to a minor mishap that landed me in these particular woods. The boxcar I had chosen was also home to a traveling bum and his dog. He was a moronic, overly hairy, ridiculously stinky bum with a mangy mutt. Patches of hair were missing from the dog and the fleas liked my flavor better then they enjoyed their original host. By the end of the first day I was covered in red itchy bumps, a cesspool of flea saliva. The bum drank Boone's Strawberry Hill nonstop from morning to night and he had a fondness for flinging his dog's feces in my general vicinity. There wasn't much I could do in this situation because the bum was larger then me by some 200 pounds and he could have easily cracked my neck. Dealing with drunken larger men was not my forte. So, I bided my time and waited for the train to slow enough so I could find another boxcar. I entertained myself with thoughts of the bum rolling off the train in a drunken stupor. I would probably still be on the train, heading for who knows where, if I hadn't decided to join the man in partaking of his favorite beverage. One night he offered me a sip and said he'd decided to quit flinging crap at me. Said he was extremely sorry and hadn't been feeling up to his old self lately, which explained his bizarre behavior. I told him not to worry. Told him I was a big girl and could take care of myself, but that I was very pleased to hear he'd quit with the shit throwing. We were getting along congenially and my woeful thoughts were turning a bit more pleasant when the foul smelling bastard decided to masturbate in front of me. Told me how lonely he got on the train and how cute I was and all sorts of oddities. This behavior went on for a few minutes. I couldn't think of a thing to do to stop it except ask, which I didn't think would work. I was proven correct in my assumption. After politely asking this shit-flinging alcoholic train hopper to take his dick elsewhere he promptly squirted me with his version of KY Jelly. Ketchup...the kind you get at fast food places. So, by this time I was covered in dry dog poop, ketchup and other bodily fluids. I was not happy and my patience was gone. I started yelling at the bum. I yelled obscenities and he quickly picked up more shit and flung it at me and then he finished his ritual and promptly threw me off the train. He told me never to come back to his boxcar. Said he never wanted to see my face again unless I brought him Strawberry Hill and was ready to party with a lonely old bum and his dog. It even managed a few barks in my direction. Then the boxcar was out of sight and I was left to pick myself up off the ground. The train hadn't been going all that fast, so I wasn't hurt, spare a scratch or two. I took notice of my surroundings and headed for the tree line. "Best not to be exposed," I whispered. All of this swam back through me as I lay there on the ground of the woods with the beast upon me. My breath was not coming back and the dog would not quit licking my body. He was all over me and I couldn't yell at him to get off. I heard nothing except the dog's tongue scratching my skin and my own disgusting thoughts of my life playing reel to reel in my mind. I lost control of the situation and the black curtain fell over my eyes.

2

"How are you feeling?" the girl asked me. "Do you feel like eating anything? I've taken the liberty of giving you some fresh clothes. We're about the same size and all." I tried to open my eyes. They felt as if someone had squeezed super glue into them and then held them shut for several hours. I moved my hand to my eyes and rubbed them every which way. Slowly they began to open. I could see the girl through the haze that clouded my eyeballs. She was actually quite beautiful with hair the color of vintage red wine and eyes of turquoise. She looked oddly familiar to me, but I was certain I had never seen her before. She repeated her question to me once again about eating. I nodded my head in a yes motion and she practically sprinted from the room only to return a few moments later with a heaping howl of spaghetti. My mouth started watering and my eyes bulged out of my head. She gave a sprite laugh and handed me the pasta. Then she propped the pillows around me and set a TV tray in front of me. I was lying in bed surrounded by pillows and all the other modern conveniences one would expect to find in the middle of the woods. I had on clean clothes and my skin no longer itched from the dried ketchup and dog shit of my earlier adventure. She noticed me noticing all of these things and smiled rather kindly. "You don't have to say anything. I realize you are tired and my Manson gave you quite a startle, didn't he? It's not often we get company out here. He is so rambunctious. He's really quite harmless though. I'm sorry he knocked the breath out of you. I didn't even notice you." She looked away, as if embarrassed, and then continued her speech. "You are feeling better, I hope? You seemed awfully tired so I let you sleep." She stood with her hands folded in front of her and a look of concern on her face. I nodded yes to her questions; I was feeling better and digging into the spaghetti. It was absolutely the best food I had consumed in approximately two weeks. 'This is great!" was all I could manage between the bites of pasta I was shoveling into my mouth. She laughed to show her approval and said when I was feeling up to it I should make myself at home. She was going out into the living room to finish her crossword puzzle and maybe later we could talk and become better acquainted. I said I would like that. She told me her name was Michelle. I swallowed a bite and told her mine was Dee. She walked toward the door and then turned and gave me a little wave. She said she liked having company and she hoped I would like it here. I thought maybe I would. I laughed to myself over her quirky personality but then I thought how I might act if I lived alone in the woods and didn't have much human contact. I'd probably act a bit giddy and goofy too. I dismissed her eccentricities and continued eating. I couldn't imagine food tasting any better than this. I finished my pasta and set the bowl on the bedside table. I laid the TV tray on the floor next to the bed and reached for the remote control. I hadn't viewed a television in months and I wondered if there was anything on. The antenna didn't pick up very many stations. I supposed living in the woods didn't help matters much. I dropped the remote on the bedcovers and closed my eyes for a moment to fully grasp my current situation. I had a good feeling about Michelle and her dog, Manson. I liked the woods and this cabin. Maybe Michelle really was my savior. I'd gotten myself in a bit of trouble before this horrid adventure of mine had taken off. Actually, my troubles are what started this ordeal. I decided not to think about all of that at the moment, so with my eyes still shut I let my thoughts carry me into dreamland. "…gory scene…seven young women…Karta Zelta Ghi…butchered with a Calico M950…one suspect not in custody at this time…still at large…back later with more details…" My eyes flew open and I was able to see the news broadcaster. She had brown eyes and brown hair and was wearing a brown outfit. Blah with brown. No wonder I couldn't get this troubling scenario out of mind. It was on television and probably in the newspapers too. The incident had happened a few short months ago. I realized to the news media this was still a hot-happening piece of journalism. "Lovely Young Sorority Girls Blasted Down by a Psycho for No Apparent Reason." It wouldn't have surprised me if the rights for book and movie deals were being negotiated right now as I lay here. I was in trouble. I had to get out of here as soon as possible. What if Michelle had been watching the news? Or perhaps she'd picked up a paper not too long ago. Surely, she'd put two and two together. But would she be so nice to me if she knew I was a butcher? I wasn't sure and I couldn't stick around to find out. I had to leave. Such was the life of one on the run. I threw the covers back and attempted to step out of bed but my mind was like a marshmallow and my limbs felt like lead weights. I couldn't discern the door from the window and the flowers were sprouting at a rapid pace from the throw rug near the bed. I tried to call Michelle's name but laughter cut the air and I stopped trying to get out of bed.

"Not only are you a murderess, a suspect that every policeman across the country would love to get their hands on, but you are also one trusting, stupid, hallucinating bitch. How do you feel, Dee? I put special mushrooms in your spaghetti." She laughed maniacally. Now I knew how one felt before the guillotine chopped off all thought. Little did I know how close to the truth I was. When I looked at Michelle again, she was still standing in the doorway, but this time she was holding a chainsaw and she was sprouting horns. I wasn't sure if my eyes were fooling me, due to the mushrooms she'd fed me, but I decided to take no chances…I leapt out of the bed as best as my weak body would allow me to. She didn't flinch at all. She started the saw and spoke in a loud voice, "So, you thought you could fool me? You thought you could fool the entire country? I know who you are. I know what you did. And believe me, seeing as how you and I are so isolated out here in these woods, you will fucking pay for what you did. I don't take kindly to strangers *gunning* down sorority girls and I especially don't take to strangers gunning down *my* little sister!" Her words hit my mind like a bullet. Her sister! Oh god, how could I have known that things would end up this way? I murdered her sister and now she was going to kill me.

3

"That's right, Dee. My little sister was a member of Karta Zelta Ghi and now she's dead!"

She was slowly approaching me and my concern for my safety was mounting. I had to think fast and I had to get out of here. I didn't come all this way to be killed by a whore's sister. I could now see the resemblance. Her sister and my ex-roommate, there was a definite correlation. It was starting to make sense to my marshmallow brain. I sank back down onto the bed. Even though the majority of my drug-using days were over I thought how much fun this might be if the circumstances were altered just a bit.

"Don't you fucking move or I'll chop your head off."

She had approached the bed and was about two inches from my face. The spittle from her mouth hit me like tiny daggers. I shut my eyes and prepared to die. She cut off the saw. Silence. No movement. I held my breath. I wasn't ready to die, but almost any fate would be a rewarding welcome. Still, nothing happened. I dared to open my eyes and quicker than I could think she had grabbed me by the hair on my head and yanked me out of the bed onto the floor. I was twisting in agony amongst the beautiful sunflowers when I began to utter silly nonsensical phrases. Her face floated above mine and her mouth twisted into an evil grimace as she placed one big combat-booted foot on my chest.

"What the hell did you just say to me, you fucking sick twisted murdering cunt?"

Her foot was causing an enormous amount of pressure on my already winded lungs. I wasn't breathing well but I tried to speak again and she slapped me on the cheek and all of my coherent thoughts flew out the window.

"Yes, that's what I thought you said," she hissed. "I suggest you stay right here and don't even plot an escape. I'm going to the phone to call my father, who'll be pleased to know I caught you. I guess that *Most Wanted* show really does work. You can thank a little old lady about 60 miles from here for your capture. She was outside watering her flowers the day you were tossed off the train. She couldn't believe her eyes. She called the show right away and we figured it wouldn't be too long before you ended up here. I'm the only human around for miles and miles and miles." She grinned as she said this, then she kicked me in the chest to make sure I wouldn't stray from my position on the floor.

I tried violently to regain control of my breath. My chest was aching from Manson knocking me down and then Michelle stepping on me. How in the hell did I always manage to get myself into these predicaments? I wish I knew, so I could avoid it. I couldn't believe the ill luck I had. And I could thank the lovely sorority bitches for all of it. I hadn't always hated sorority girls. I acknowledged them, but stayed away, for their beliefs were not my own. When I was eighteen years old I applied to Karta Zelta Ghi because my parents thought it would do me some good. They thought it would give me some sort of direction. They didn't like the path I had chosen, that path of dyed-hair freaks and tattooed punks. They didn't like the artsy farts I chose to hold in high regard. The sorority was the only way they knew to revamp my life. I agreed to apply to avoid the arguments I knew would follow if I disobeyed. I was accepted and moved in for the school term. The whole time I was packing I was sure there had been some sort of mistake. Perhaps my parents were playing some cruel joke on me. I honestly didn't think a sorority was going to show me any direction. Upon moving in I discovered that my roommate was a complete whore. She'd have a different guy over every other night of the week. I was forced to find quieter studying places and sometimes even quieter sleeping arrangements. No matter how much I tried to stifle her noises, I could still hear exactly what was going on. Most nights I fell asleep with my headphones on, the music pulsating my brain at a rather audible level. She'd have the gall to complain that my industrial music was keeping her awake! Most of the other girls and I didn't get along. I fancied myself a poet and I scurried around the campus scribbling in many different notebooks. My sisters didn't understand my behavior but I was undaunted. My parents suggested I start a poetry reading night at the house. They thought maybe we could find common ground. I thought it sounded plausible. I was hoping it would give them an understanding of me. But they couldn't manage much more than rhyming cat and bat so I gave up on a lost cause. I did my best to avoid these creatures I lived with. It was working for a time. But one day I returned from class to my room and noticed all of my notebooks were missing. I was furious. I set about destroying the entire house. I upheaved everything looking for my notebooks. My life was in those notes. My thoughts, my convictions, my life. They had taken everything I held dear and they tried to convince me I had misplaced my things. They tried to convince me I was neurotic, that I was going insane. They couldn't win me over to their world and they couldn't leave me alone. They tortured me silently with their pitiful looks. They were mad because I refused to conform. They were mad because I had the balls to do my own thing. They called my parents and told them I had been stealing large amounts of money from the sorority treasure chest and had been caught doing lines of coke in the community bathroom and when confronted by them I had talked of suicide. They told my parents I had destroyed the house and locked myself in my room. That part was true. I needed a safe place. I had none. My parents showed up the next day and drove me straight to the loony bin slash rehab center. They wouldn't even listen to my side of the story. They were sure I was simply in denial They wanted me to be like everyone else and it saddened them so, to see me end this way. My parents moved and left no forwarding address. I never saw them again. Six months of my life were stolen from me. My parents were ripped from my life. The ones I blamed resided at Karta Zelta Ghi. When I was released I went there and I stole the life from every one of those evil girls. I couldn't seem to help myself. I could see her shadow on the wall in the other room. I knew if I didn't move I would die. I slowly crawled across the floor to the chainsaw she had left there. I leaned against the wall by the door and waited for her to return. Maybe if I was lucky I could maim her enough to make my escape. It would be difficult. I heard her footsteps approach the door and my body tensed in apprehension of what I was about to do. She wasn't fooled.

"Dee, you can drop the fucking saw. I know where I left it and it isn't there. I know you have it."

The saw dropped with a thud. As she stomped into the room she was carrying a teakettle and several rags. Steam was swarming out of the top of the kettle. I thought it a bit ironic that we would be having a tea party at this time. My thoughts turned morbid and my imagination ran away with the possibilities of what she could do to me. I didn't like what I was thinking and without a second thought I once again made a grab for the saw. I started it and made a sweep at her ankles. I was hoping to chop them off but she saw me coming and jumped. The hot water from the kettle spilled down the front of her body and with an agonizing scream she threw the kettle at my head and then she fell to the floor. I was able to duck out of the way of the flying kettle and I winced as it hit the wall. Michelle was clutching her legs, which were turning a bright red, and she screamed, "*Fuck! Fuck you!*"

I made a quick decision and took my weak tripping ass right out the front door of the cabin. I didn't want to be around if and when her father showed up. Manson jumped up as if prepared to follow me and even though I thought about stealing her dog, I decided I didn't want to deal with any more canines. I told him to "stay" praying he knew that command. I remembered what way I had entered the woods so I ran in the opposite direction. I wanted to find the ocean. I vowed that someday I would return for Michelle and I would seek my revenge on her. The whole family was rotten. She wanted me dead. She knew who I was and what I had done. If that wasn't reason alone to seek revenge then I didn't know what was. The days pass quickly now. Time was such an abstract idea to me. It was totally amazing how I could sit in the same exact spot from the time the sun came up in the morning until it went down at night and do absolutely nothing. I spent day after day like this until somehow I felt as though I was going to spontaneously combust. I mentally shut my mind's eye and waited and waited and waited some more. At the present moment I was hunched up against a tree and I was waiting for the sun to come up so I could continue my search for the ocean. I could smell the salt on the winds. I knew I was close. California was weird that way. You could step out of the forest and walk onto a beach. I'd grown up in Texas and the areas around Galveston and Padre Island, which were not like that. I'd seen a seagull a couple of hours ago. Or maybe it was a couple of days ago. Like I said, time was an abstract idea.

    I'd dragged some brush together and formed a little shelter, and I was staying comfortably warm, considering where I was and what I was going through. I turned inward and thought of my mother. I recalled a story she had told me long ago about her and her hippie daze. She'd been chain smoking joint after joint with some other friends. Music was going and the smoke was floating and Mom looks over and sees these two praying mantises fucking. It's a documented fact that the female mantis will promptly bite the head off the male during the sex act. This helps her control the male and after sex he dies. Mom decided to heighten their groovy experience and blow some Dot smoke in the general vicinity of the two copulating bugs.... She kept a close vigil and noticed the insects were slowing down, and then when they finished, instead of beheading her mate the female mantis went one way and the male, head intact, went his. I guess there is no point to this story except the thought of fucking and the thought of my mom were two distinctive, yet comforting, feelings.

    I had been through a completely disdainful hell the last few months. I really didn't like killing people. Torture was nice. It's always good to see the look of terror in their eyes. But killing was so...brutal...Neanderthal...permanent. Fuck those bitches! I really do hate sorority girls. The whole idea of a group of girls who couldn't think for themselves appalled me. Nobody understood my thoughts so I was forced to hop a train and get fucked over by a bum.

I turned over in my little bed of dirt and twigs and brush. I prayed these aimless days of wandering would lead me to the ocean floor. I prayed the nightmares would stay at bay, far away from my mind, but I wasn't sure my prayers would be answered. I had to face facts and Murphy was my god.

I awaken to rude jostling. Mutters and grunts fill the air. Branches are scraping my body and I feel a kick to my stomach. Breathless, I open my eyes and *holy fucking terror!* She is here. She has found me. She is muttering wild fantastical things to me, talk about killing me, talk about cutting off my toes so I can't run away. *Jesus fuck!!* How in the world did she find me? I pretend it's a dream, but when her foot connects to my stomach again, I know I must face reality. She grabs me by the feet and drags me through the woods. Dirt and gravel get in my mouth. She lifts me as best as she can and pushes me into the trunk of her car. I know I'm screwed. My reality is now a nightmare.

She must have been searching for a while. Surely it had taken me several days to get this far. I was near the ocean. I was so confused. I'm in the trunk now and she is looking down at me with a leering grin. She is breathing hard from her exertion. My head is spinning and voices are muffled and I can't breathe. I feel blood running down my face so I touch it. There is definitely blood on my hand. I hold it out to show her and she laughs. I manage to kick her in the chest from my position in the trunk. She curses at me and slams the trunk shut. I hear a car door shut and the engine starts. The car jerks forward and I'm thrown back and forth inside the trunk. Nightmare becomes reality once again. It's dark and the trunk stinks. I'm beyond disoriented and I'm bleeding from my head....

We had been driving for a considerable amount of time and my body was beginning to cramp. I could feel bruises growing on my limbs. I had no idea where the ocean was or the woods or her cabin. The mental map I had drawn was gone, seeping out of my head with the blood. I thought maybe my head had quit bleeding but I wasn't certain. I guess this was it. I was going to be killed and dumped in the woods and my life would be over. The car suddenly screeched to a halt and my head slammed against more metal, starting the flow of blood back up. Now, if I did manage to get out of this alive, she would truly pay for my wrath. Only problem was, I didn't quite know how to get out of this mess. I could try to take her by surprise when she opened the trunk but that seemed impossible. She would be expecting that. I could play dead. I felt dead. I was bleeding and cold and tired and pissed off. That constituted "dead" in my mind. I didn't have much time to prepare though because the trunk lid popped and the adventure was about to begin.

"Don't you dare try anything, you fucking cunt."

I heard this as the trunk lid popped. That decided it for me. I would play dead like the possum before the rabid dog. I could hear footsteps approach the back of the car. They stopped. Not one pair, but two or more. Did she have a fucking army with her? Jesus...I was really screwed. The lid was opened a bit. Nothing. I dared to squint my eyes open the tiniest bit and almost dropped a load right there. I could see her body and one other and a .357 Magnum being pointed at my head. I told myself to remain calm. If I remained calm I could get out of this mess. I took several deep breaths, as much as my wounded body would allow me to. With my eyes still squinted partly open I realized the hand holding the gun belonged to a police officer. I'd seen the uniform but it hadn't clicked until this particular moment. Holy shit! What the fuck was I supposed to do? I closed my eyes when I heard his voice.

"Well, well, well..." he drawled with an almost fake southern accent. "So, this is the murdering little whore you found lost out in the woods, huh, Michelle? The murdering little whore who killed your sister?"

When he spoke my horror intensified. This was the cop from every stereotypical movie I'd ever seen, that evil bastard who preyed on the weak, unsuspecting, undeserving victim. I knew I was in for some unpleasant experiences.

"Yes, Dad, that's her. She was sneaking up on my cabin but Manson caught her just in time. He knocked her down and stayed on her chest until I could find my chainsaw. I'm not sure what would have happened had Manson not been with me. Maybe she would have killed me too."

I couldn't believe the sleazy fucked up fortune Murphy so kindly bestowed upon me. Not only did I kill this bitch's sister, but I also killed a cop's daughter and the cop was crooked. My closed eyes rolled back in my head. I said a silent "fuck you" prayer to my god and continued playing dead. Murphy always said if it could go wrong it would.

I could feel his breath on me. He apparently was leaning into the trunk. I lay perfectly still. His breath stank of coffee and cigarettes. It had that stale lingering quality about it. I imagined him kissing his wife and I wondered if she had left him by now. My head reverberated with canned laughter. But god, his breath did stink. I wasn't sure if I'd be able to contain myself for much longer. He didn't say anything for a long time. I wasn't able to open my eyes for fear of ruining my possum routine so I simply lay there.

"Get your ass out of the car, nice and slow like..." click, "and don't try anything funny unless you enjoy cold metal

bullets coursing through your body."
I lay there. The barrel of the gun nudged deep into my right nostril. Hey there. I was imagining his finger pulling the trigger. It was a welcome thing. It had to be better then this fateful punishment I was receiving. I wasn't a quitter, but the situation I was in seemed impossible to get out of.

"We got a bitch trying to be a possum. What do you think we should do, Michelle?"

Michelle said nothing. I braced myself for what I was sure would be next and sure enough they proved my second guessing abilities were still intact. The gun exploded...but not at me. It was a scare tactic. It didn't work, because I knew it was coming. I lay perfectly still. By some miracle of Murphy, I lay still and I could breathe. Incredible disbelief seeped through me as cop man said, "Well, I'll be damned. The bitch ain't playing possum after all."

Fingers grabbed my hair. Suddenly the fingers let go and the pig squealed. "She's hurt. Damn, there's a lot of blood. She must be passed out cold. Oh well, this can only make my job easier. Fucking cunt is gonna pay for what she's done."

And with the end of this statement, I was literally flung out of the trunk. I hit the ground so hard, my body involuntarily grunted. I managed to keep my pain in check and I didn't move.

"Dad! Did you hear that? She is playing possum. Kick her and see what she does."

"I ain't gonna kick her, Michelle. I've seen enough head injuries to know that she really is passed out cold. I've got something planned out real good for her." He let out a holler of joy and then continued, "Now, you go on around the other side of the car there and you are my lookout. Whistle real loud if you see anyone come around, ya hear me?"

I was thinking Michelle must always do what Daddy says because she made no complaint. I was dragged about four feet away from the car and my pants were ripped off of my body. I could hear a zipper being unzipped slowly, deliberately, and I heard his gnawing laughter fill the air. I knew what was coming now. It was going to take all of my concentration not to kick him in the nuts. But I reminded myself he had the gun and that focused me on remaining still. If only I could get away while still alive.... He crawled upon me like a fat fucking walrus. I didn't dare move or make a sound. The butt of the gun rested against my right nostril. I wanted to shout at him. I wanted to tell him he was a left-handed inbred fucking slobbery pig but I didn't dare. I kept my mouth shut and my thoughts subdued, my survival instincts swimming clumsily, refusing to drown. I had no escape plan. I had no one to help me. I felt things around my pelvis. I felt hands groping and digging and I made my mind a black spiraling void on purpose. I didn't want to know. I just wanted this to be over. I heard sucking noises and grunts and I thought of big fat hog at the trough. I gagged but he didn't seem to notice. His face was very near to mine and I could smell the stale breath once again. This horrible apparition on top of me was permeating and gagging all of my senses. I didn't know how to make this stop. His face came very close to mine and he was grunting unintelligible things in my ear. I took a chance and opened my eyes a tiny bit to scope out my surroundings. I could see the cop's head out of my peripheral vision. He had his shirt off and his back was very hairy. It was dipping up and down in a sporadic motion. I looked the other direction and I saw the car. I couldn't see Michelle. And as if in answer to my thought, she whistled. Holy fucking yes! A whistle meant someone was coming. Cop man stopped his dirty business and started cussing obscenities, obviously displeased for being interrupted. The thought crossed my mind to holler for help, but no sooner had I thought this then his boot kicked me in the head and my torture was over.

4

Drifting into my subconscious, I couldn't discern reality from fantasy. I vaguely recalled being flung around like a bag of garbage. Pig had rooted throughout the trough. I opened my eyes a sliver and noticed how bright the sun was. But as I looked down upon my helpless skeletal frame, I noticed shadows. I took a closer look at what I assumed was the sun and I saw instead walls—yellow walls. I attempted to move my head a bit and noticed I was in some sort of shelter. Yellow walls...shadows...shelter... Yellow walls of a school bus stand out clearly now. A school bus on the sand seemed a bit preposterous but I allowed this thought to focus. It couldn't be any more preposterous then anything else I'd experienced lately. This school bus had been abandoned on the beach. The windows had been broken out and the wind made a terrible howling sound. I needed a painkiller. It was sunny out. I could hear the waves. They were trying to crash around the bus. They couldn't get in and I heard them gnash their teeth as they went back out to sea. My mind was exploding with all of the possible methods there were to kill a person. The torturous thoughts made me smile in spite of the pain. I could barely move, so the mental pictures were all I had to soothe the gnawing pain. I imagine I am calling for help. The phone rings. I answer. The party on the other end is muttering "moose" over and over again. I hang up. The overrated cliché, "escape is futile," pops into my mind. It fit my scenario with a perfect simplicity. I toss. I turn. The sand is uncomfortable. I feel a sand crab climbing up my leg. I go to brush it off and notice I do not have any pants on. I notice a sticky substance on my hand and at first I think of the word "ketchup" but I know this is wrong and I think instead of "blood." Blood is oozing out of my crotch. I feel it trying to come out of my head. I hear a barking dog. It was like the time the stinky old bum on the train had told me about being stranded on an alcove of the beach during high tide. His dog, that was busy barking at imaginary people in the cliffs, awakened him. The moon was out and he could hear the mighty roar of the waves and he could hear his dog barking in vain to be heard over the great white thunder water. Well, that's precisely what that dog sounded like to me. It was outside the walls of the bus barking and barking. I thought I was imagining things though, because surely if there was a dog, it would have sniffed me out. And a dog on the beach generally meant its master was somewhere near. And a master being near would mean I had been rescued, but since I was still in the bus, lying on the sand, half-naked, I assumed I was imagining the whole thing. I was probably imagining the bus too. I had no idea how I'd gotten in this predicament. I fade in and I fade out of consciousness. The pig from before is on top of me once again. He smells of shit. His tongue is licking me. He is furry and dark. I wonder if his wife shaves his back. I don't like cops. I hate fur. I hate me. I'm holding knives. I'm looking in the mirror. I see those damn sorority girls, spaghetti stains all over their clothes. I see their perfectly tied hair bows. I see blood spattering and I see a boy I once knew.

We were lounging on the bed, as was our custom. He pulled a knife out from under the pillow. He handed it to me and gave me explicit instructions on how to use it. I followed them carefully, for fear if I screwed up, he'd cut me. I didn't like to be cut. He did. He was into that bloodletting thing, and there were many scars to prove it. I used to lay my head upon his scarred chest and listen to his stories. My fingers would lightly trace the scars. Every scar he had signified a past lover. The night he handed me the knife I knew it was my turn to make a notch in his proverbial bedpost. I sliced his skin. I did it quick. At first there was no trace of blood. His eyes were closed and he let out a moan. Before the sound was over the blood arrived. He told me to lick it, to suck his blood. He pushed my open mouth on top of the cut. It tasted rather sweet, yet metallic. I sucked for a long time. I had a part of him now. His core, his very being, raced through my veins. I was lying on top of him. We were both naked. I could tell he was turned on, aroused by the thought of me drinking his blood. We both fell asleep—just the two of us forever locked in that moment. Holding each other while the sun came up…the bus was the same color as the sun.

I was so hot. I was covered in sand and these bizarre dream sequences continued to plague me. I could hear voices now. I couldn't make out what they were saying. The waves crashed around my mind. They washed out some of the impurities. My suicidal thoughts vanished with the outgoing tide. The murderous thoughts of before multiplied and I welcomed them. I would find that bitch. I would chop her skull off and bury pieces of the bones in the sand I'd invite the seagulls to pick away her eyeballs. I'd throw a flesh party for the sand crabs and I'd be master of ceremonies. They could eat as much as they wanted. And with microphone in hand, I'd cackle with laughter at the thought of dumb Michelle inside all those oceanic animals. Then after watching her skull disintegrate I would chop off her legs, and with each bloody torturous blow, I would yell obscenities into the wind. I would toss her bleeding stumps as far as I could into the outgoing waves and I would hide behind the sand dunes and view the innocent swimmers as they stumbled upon the legs. Aaahh…the glory! The absolute putrid glory. Putrescence at its finest.

I was a disgusting human. But then, I remembered all the grief I suffered and to hell with her like all the rest. To hell with them all! The sand felt rough on my hands. I was attempting to dig a hole to escape the cop who was once again upon me. His tongue was now scraping my face. His breath however smelled more of decayed crabs and seaweed. I couldn't escape this and the voice told me it would be O.K. They were laughing and I tried to speak but all I could manage was unintelligible words. I opted for silence. I felt hands on my body. A face made its way into my line of vision. I could make out two red eyes staring into my thoughts and the creature spoke in a snake-like whisper. As it spoke, a black tongue shot out of its mouth and smacked me right in the lips. I tried to scream but when I opened my mouth to so do, the tongue jabbed its way in and went down my throat. I thought Michelle and Manson were back for me. I groaned. I was ready to die. I could see figures floating above me and I could hear small chuckles over the waves. I was choking and gasping for air and there was a bright light in my face and I thought…this is it. I'm dead for sure now. I'm seeing the white light at the end of the tunnel. Something in my brain clicked, however, and I refused to give up. I struggled and with a tremendous yank I freed myself from the pig. I freed myself from Manson and I freed myself from Michelle. I felt a tongue licking my leg and I dared to look down. To my utter amazement there was a huge brown dog licking the sand from my body. The garish light had been removed from my eyes so I could now see. Only I wasn't sure what exactly it was that I was seeing.

"Don't mind the boxer. Mattie's just too friendly for her own good. I swear, she couldn't and wouldn't hurt a fly."

The tall boy was fairly handsome and as I turned toward his voice I noticed it did not reek of stale air. The cop was no longer on top of me and Michelle was nowhere to be seen. I looked around and noticed a midget puffing on a cigarette. He took off his coat and extended it out to me and said, "I'm Sam."

His cigarette was dangling from his mouth and he puffed on it like that was his only joy in life. I took the coat and only then did I remember that I was naked from the waist down. I laid the coat over me and smiled in a grateful gesture. He then reached into his pocket and offered me a cigarette.

I took it and said, "Thanks. My name is Dee."

I looked at the other boy and he said his name was Jake. Then he sat down on the sand and motioned for Sam to do the same.

"We tried to catch the people hurting you. We were out driving around and noticed a guy in a cop's uniform gyrating all over the sand. Then we saw you. We honked the horn and stepped on the gas and then this girl popped up from in front of the car and both she and the cop headed for the doors. They jumped in and roared off. We followed them for a while and since we couldn't catch them we came back for you. But when we returned, you weren't there. We searched for a few minutes and then we climbed over a sand dune and there was Mattie running around the bus and darting in and out. Do you want to tell me how all of this happened? I think we can help you. We have a bit of a personal interest in this particular situation." He looked at Sam and winked, and in response, Sam took a drag on his smoke.

"Well, it's a really long story. The girl held me hostage and then I escaped. She eventually found me and next thing I know I'm getting plowed by a pig. Then, I passed out and I don't know what happened. I was having some bad dreams about chanting voices and black snakes. Then I woke up."

I shrugged. I didn't want to tell them everything for fear they would turn me in to the authorities. I was having a hard time trusting anyone.

"Well, I suppose it's my turn. We have an interest because the cop that was harming you turned out to be the same one who murdered our friend's father. We adopted Darla and we've been trying to locate the bastard. Thanks to you, we now know precisely where he lives, or at least where the people he associates with live. We followed the two all the way to this cabin in the woods."

I gasped suddenly and Jake stopped his speech.

"I know where that cabin is, too. That's where she held me hostage. Her name is Michelle."

Jake was quiet for a moment, munching on the new information I'd just supplied him with. Then when he spoke, he did so to Sam. "We are going to help her. We can finally nail this dick. The others won't mind."

Then he turned to me and said, "You are coming with us. We're going to help you."

I just nodded my head in agreement and Mattie came over and laid her head in my lap. She licked a few spots of blood off my inner thighs. We sat there for a few brief moments and then Jake said the car wasn't far from here. I stood up and wrapped Sam's coat around my waist and we headed off over the sand dune in the direction of the car.

5

We pulled up to the front of a little bar called Smiley's. Jake said we were within walking distance of the house but one of their roommates worked here and they just wanted to pick up some food and tell the roomie they had a new member in the house. I said I would wait in the car since I didn't have pants and didn't much feel like being out in public. They understood and said they would be back in a minute. While they were inside, I took the opportunity to examine my new surroundings.

The town was a picturesque scene, from the Norman Rockwell days. It was the sort of town that thrived in the summer. The houses were close together and weathered and the lawns were well manicured. The majority of these houses had white picket fences. It was the perfect spot to retire to when old age set in. There was a main road where a post office resided and a small convenience store where all the basic necessities could be bought. The people walking around on the main street appeared friendly enough and most of them had on sunbathing apparatus. I assumed the ocean was at the end of the main street. We hadn't actually driven all the way to the end of it, but the people dressed for the ocean were all walking in the same direction.

While I was busy daydreaming about the sea, a car pulled up next to Jake's and out piled three sorority-type girls and two jock frat boys. I only stereotyped them because of the way their high- pitched giggles hurt my ears. I gave them a cursory glance, my disdain showing plainly on my face. The look did not go unnoticed. When the kids piled out of the car, one of the doors hit Jake's. I shot them a nasty look at that particular moment, but I had no energy to do anything about the situation. The boy who had flung open the door peered into the car and shot me a snide look that said "what you gonna do about it?" and then he proceeded inside the bar, laughing all the way. I watched them walk hand in hand, their pretentious attitude tainting the air of Balinas Bay.

I took a quick look around to see if anyone was out on the streets to hear witness to my plan of action. Apparently everyone was swimming for the streets were uncrowded. I stole out of the car and took a peek inside the bowhead's vehicle. It was a typical clutter of CD cases, clothes, schoolbooks and hair bows. "Shit," I muttered under my breath. I was amused in a sadistic sort of way. I tried one of the doors, but it was locked. I tried the next one and it opened with ease. I jumped in and shut the door so I wouldn't arouse suspicion. I was looking for some pants to wear. First things first. It took me a while to find what I was looking for. I dug through some gaudy '70s wannabe plaid polyester pants. I refused to wear them. I thanked Murphy for their taste in clothing. Apparently they shopped at thrift stores because it was the cool hip thing to do. I shopped at thrift stores because it was the affordable thing to do. And with pants like these in the car I knew they were leaving me all the good stuff. Finally I found a decent pair of brown cords that only needed a pair of scissors taken to the hems. I slipped them on and then I got back into Jake's car. I wanted to leave a token of my thanks. I found a pen and a piece of paper and I hurriedly scribbled out a note. "Thanks for the brown cords. It pays for the dent your asshole jock frat fuck left in my friend's car door. Have a great fucking day, bitch!" Once again I slipped out of Jake's car, glanced around me, and seeing no one, I let the air out of all the tires and then I dropped the note on her seat. I jumped back into Jake's car and waited for my friends to come back out, a smug smile filling my face.

6

I was watching the front door of Smiley's waiting for the clones to return when Jake and Sam came out carrying a couple bags of food and Sam was drinking a beer. I realized how badly I wanted a beer. I was hoping they had more. They got in the car to tell me Smiley would be driving home tonight so we were going to leave the car there. The house was close, so I stepped out. Jake noticed right away I had pants on. He held out a pair to me and laughingly said, "I found these in the back of the bar. Darla left them here and they looked like they might fit. But I guess you don't need them now." He winked at me and told me he hoped I was hungry because they'd bought burgers for everyone. Big fat drippy juicy burgers! I told him I'd eat one only if they ate my actual burger because I didn't like meat. They both decided that wouldn't be a problem. We headed toward the back of the bar, around the side and out the little white picket fence. We crossed an alley and started walking down the street. Jake said it was time he elaborated on the story of Darla. I shook my head in an O.K. motion and looked toward Sam as he offered me a cigarette. I took it and then grabbed a bag of food to look for the beers.

"Darla came to us when she was six years old. I found her on the streets of San Francisco. She was wandering around Golden Gate Park at the end of Haight Street. She had this wild look in her eyes. I had just gotten off the bus and stepped into the McDonald's there and ordered some food. I was looking out the window when I saw her. She appeared to be alone and lost. I grabbed my food and headed out the door, across the street. I have a soft spot for kids. Some of them are just never given a chance in life and I'm sort of a little kid underdog."

We took a right at the next street we came to and we continued walking. The beach was only a few blocks away now and the smell of salt tickled my nose.

"So, I got over to her side of the street and as I locked my eyes upon her I noticed she was staring directly into mine. When I asked her if she was alone she shook her head yes. She said her daddy wouldn't wake up." Jake stopped talking for a minute and then he turned toward me and said, "I really fucking hate little kids being left to fend for themselves in this brutal fucking world." He continued walking and he said Darla took him to the place where her Daddy was. "It was a rundown building and I had a feeling she'd been camping out for awhile to know exactly where it was located. We went up some stairs and weaved our way through a maze of rickety junk. It was an abandoned building except for the bugs and rodents. Her father was lying on top of a pile of newspapers. It was obvious to me that he was dead and that he had been dead for quite some time. Rigor mortis had a good grip on him. His lips were purple and his eyes were shut but rolled back into his head. As I looked down at her father's body, I was unnerved. He stunk of death, and even though she didn't say it, I think Darla was very aware that he was gone. I decided then and there she would be my child. I wasn't about to leave her in the clutches of the system. So I took her with me."

His words sunk deep into my heart. "What happened to her dad?" I questioned.

Jake shrugged his shoulders and said, "I found some needles near his body. I assumed he was an OD case. I found out later it was murder. There was an article in the paper about him. And then later, I got into some trouble and one night while I was in jail I overheard a cop talking about him. My ears perked up and I almost lost my mind when they said another cop had killed him. They never said why, but it didn't matter to me. A fucking filthy pig had jacked off another innocent behind the officials' backs and he'd gotten away with it. I decided then and there I would seek revenge on him. And as it turns out now I have an even deeper reason to hurt that beast. He was the one hurting you."

He hung his head as he continued walking. I took a swig of beer. There was a lot of information to suck down and I was having a hard time. I was still in pain. I was still hungry. We reached a gate in the row of fences and Jake stepped into a tiny yard. He looked toward me and jokingly asked where I got the pants. I started laughing so hard some of the beer shot out of my nose. We found ourselves in the doorway, stepping into the house in a cloud of good comfortable humor, laughing all the way. This is how I first met Darla.

7

She looked to be fourteen years old. She had long hair that had been dyed a violet black color. Her eyes were ice blue. She was the most amazing creature my eyes had ever laid upon. I was struck with a sense of angelic pureness.

I reached my hand toward her and said, "Hi, I'm Dee. You must be Darla."

Her hand melted into mine and she drew me close to give me a hug. I was taken aback by her openness and comfort around me, after just meeting me. Strange thing was, I felt the same toward her. Jake handed her the bag of food he was hogging and he went to the fridge to put the beer away. He kept three out and grabbed lemonade Snapple for Darla.

We didn't speak as we were getting our food ready. Instead, everyone was so hungry, when I chanced to take a peek around me at these loving strangers, all their eyes were on the burgers. I peeled my patty off and handed it to Jake. He sneered at Sam and stuck the whole patty on his burger. I silently laughed.

Their attitude toward each other was that of longtime friends, or else friends that had been through much together in a short amount of time. I was a bit curious about this, so I posed a question to Jake. "I wanna know how you two met."

Jake quit chewing, as if pondering this thought, and then swallowed the burger in his mouth down with a swig of beer. He looked at Sam and said, "Do you mind?"

Sam shook his head no and pulled the old familiar smoke out of his pocket. I was amazed that he could smoke and eat at the same time.

Jake put his burger down and began the story by leaning back in his chair. He grabbed his beer, put his feet on the table and said, "I saved Sam's ass from some cops. Some lady was getting mugged on the ferry that was headed for Alcatraz island. Sam jumped in between the old woman and the mugger and managed to scare him off. Well, the old lady was so scared that she continued screaming. The guards on the ferry managed to arrive on the scene just as Sam was jumping up and down, screaming back at the lady. She was too damn noisy and the sound was hurting his ears. Well, the cops thought Sam was mugging her so they beat him down and that's when I stepped in. I was strolling along, seeing the sights when I look a little ways down the ferry and see this old woman screaming at this midget. I thought it looked like an interesting scenario so I decided to check it out. When I got closer they were..."

Sam, who had jumped up on his chair, beer in one hand, cigarette in the other, began shouting, "I hate those damn cops to this day too. They had me this fucking close to the ground." He put his nose flat against the table. In a barely audible whisper he said, "Then they started bashing my head into the ferry's floor." With this silent proclamation he began beating his head against the table, two, three, four times. And just as suddenly as this outburst started, it stopped. "Fucking filthy pigs! Death to murdering, rapist cops! "He straightened up and without taking notice of any of us, he hopped down off the chair and sauntered out of the room.

Jake got up from the table and helped himself to another beer from the fridge. He looked at the clock above the stove and said, "Smiley should be home soon. He said he was closing early tonight. He can calm Sam down. He's the only one who can. But that's how we met. I managed to convince the pigs he was helping the old bat."

I nodded at Jake and said it did indeed answer my question. I told him I had another one. He laughed and begged me to ask. "Well, didn't we stop at Smiley's bar earlier? And if so, is Smiley your roommate?"

His eyes twinkled as he noticed my confusion. "He is our roommate. In fact, he owns this house. When his children moved out, he was lonely. So, he asked us all to move in and keep him company. We agreed, and ever since, we've been one big smiling happy family."

And at that moment the back door that leads into the kitchen sprang open and in walked Smiley. Or at least I assumed it was Smiley. He was a short gray-haired man with a huge polident grin on his face. He came right over to me and bellowed my name like we were long lost friends. He wrapped his short stocky old man arms around me and gave me a hug that lifted me off the floor.

"Welcome to the family, Dee. I hope you like it here. Jake and Sam and Darla are some good kids. They told me you ran into some trouble and I know they can help you out of it."

His smile dominated the room and pretty soon all of us were grinning. It was the strangest feeling, all this smiling. I had the suspicion that I was gonna like it here. He said I must be tired after my little adventure and he suggested that Darla show me the bedroom I'd be staying in. She took my hand and led me down the hall. She was a quiet child and for the moment this suited me just fine. I had so much new information to process that I would have been quite daft at the art of conversation.

We stopped at a door in the long hallway and Darla opened the door. "Here's your room. There's a bathroom that connects and I've given you some of my clothes to wear until we can get you some clean ones of your own. I think you'll be quite comfortable here. Do you like the ocean, Dee?"

"I love the ocean. I want to see it tomorrow. I've loved the ocean since I was young. We used to vacation there when I was a little girl. My mom and my dad..." I stopped and swung around to her and put my hands on her head and whispered that I was sorry.

She didn't say anything, but instead she put her arms around me and said it was O.K. It didn't matter anymore. We stood like that for a few moments, silent, pondering each other. Then she released me and said it was time for her to go to bed. I nodded my goodnights and gave her a final hug. Then she left and I stood surveying my surroundings.

The room had belonged to a girl. There were pictures everywhere of cats and horses. There were some trophies that looked to be from a rodeo. This girl must have been a horse rider. I wondered where she was and if she still rode horses. The walls were painted in purple and red, bright happy colors. I loved this room. I went into the bathroom and started some hot bathwater. I went to the closet and found a robe. This would do for the night. It was big and thick and warm looking. I slid into the bathtub and the water flowed over me like massaging fingers. I could feel tensions escaping. I could feel wounds healing. I could think of nothing but peaceful thoughts.

8

I lay in the tub for a long time. I was thinking and wondering about the sudden turn of events. I thought about Jake and how I was mildly attracted to him. I thought about Darla and how fucking cute she was. I'd always had a thing for little kids but she was more in the category of sister than anything else. I thought about Smiley and how absolutely wonderful he was for taking all these people in. I thought about Sam. All the thoughts swirled together. I wondered why I had felt the urge to kill those sorority girls and why I had acted upon that urge. I let the water soothe my body as well as soothe my mind. I drifted off into a peaceful float mood and thought of absolutely nothing.

I was having a great time being alone when I was interrupted by voices. They were chanting. They sounded familiar. I couldn't place them. I decided it was time to get out of the tub and go lay down. I needed a good night's sleep. Maybe the voices were in my own head. I was getting semi-used to hearing things lately. All the traumatic events I'd swirled through lately would definitely lend a hand in the ever-growing shadow of voices I'd been hearing.

I reached the bed and had just laid my head on the pillow when the voices came again. The more I listened, the more I realized it was coming from outside. The sound of the waves mixed with the voices. I couldn't discern what they were saying through my foggy mind and the noise of the waves. I crawled out of bed and went over to the window. The moonlight was perfect to see by. I noticed the backyard was quiet and I walked through the house, but all was normal. The noises were coming from outside. I headed for the front door. I was careful to be quiet so I wouldn't wake anyone in the house. I guess I'd fallen asleep in the tub. I checked the clock on my way through the kitchen and to my surprise I noticed I had indeed been asleep for several hours. I was so relaxed in the tub I didn't even notice time passing away.

I headed out the front door and right away I noticed this front yard was different than most. This front yard was actually a deck. The deck was connected to a staircase. I couldn't see where it went but I could hear the voices and the waves much better out here. I headed for the stairs. In amazement, I looked down, way down, and these stairs went all the way down to the ocean. Smiley's house was on a high cliff. It must have been at least 50 feet down to the beach. And that's where the noises were coming from. I could see the outline of a group of people. They were all dressed in similar dark clothing. Their voices were rising up to me. An image popped into my mind. A line from a Nick Cave song floated through my brain. "There's a devil crawling across the floor." All these people were out on the beach in the middle of the night and I felt like I shouldn't be watching. I couldn't decide if I should go get Jake or if I should just go back to bed. Then I noticed a figure that looked suspiciously like Sam. I watched as he went over to a spot on the beach and picked up a package of some kind. It looked bulky and heavy. He held it toward the moon and over the sound of the sea I could hear Sam's 'voice. *"Death to the pigs!"*

I decided I'd seen enough and heard enough, if they had wanted me to know they were out there, they would have invited me to come along. I turned to climb the few stairs I had just descended. Upon reaching them I looked down at the beach one more time and I noticed someone out in the waves. Someone else was leaving the water. I began to think the figure out in the ocean looked like Darla when her voice confirmed it. She was calling for Jake. And then the figure leaving the water stopped and he turned and I knew there was something indeed strange going on. I didn't really like myself for snooping and spying in this manner but I wanted to know what was going on. I lived here now, didn't I? Why were they keeping secrets from me? What was going on? I noticed Jake leaving the water now. The moon was so bright. I was now able to make out more of the party on the beach. I saw Smiley. He was busy building a fire. Jake walked over to him and Sam met him there, dragging the heavy package behind him. Jake took the package from Sam and threw it onto the fire. It illuminated the figures on the beach. There were three people there I didn't know. The fire grew and crept up into the night sky. I could hear the package crackling and hissing. I looked toward Darla and she was waving her arms about and dancing wildly in the breaking surf. I continued my vigil of the strange scene taking place before me. The others had gathered around the fire and were now holding hands and chanting. The old familiar voices were still there.

I decided it was time to quit my spying. But before I could get out of sight, I noticed Sam pointing up the stairs in my general vicinity. I ducked out of sight, cussing myself for being seen. I couldn't be certain if they had seen me, but I couldn't figure out any other reason for Sam to be pointing. I had lost face in front of them. They would probably throw me out in the streets, to fend Michelle off in my own terms. I ran across the deck and entered the front door, careful to leave everything as it had been. I ran toward my room and did a nervous little dance from the bed to my window back to the bed again. I crawled into the bed and pulled the covers up over my head. The thought of losing these new friends was more awful then the thought of spending the rest of my natural born life in jail for killing those sorority bitches. I let out a moan and tried to think of something to say if and when I was confronted for spying. All I really wanted to do was die.

9

Breakfast.

I could smell it.

Bacon, biscuits, orange juice. Even though I didn't eat meat, there was something about the way frying bacon smelled that set my glands to salivating. As if on cue, a knock at my door.

"C'mon in," I chirped.

The door opened and Darla appeared wearing a smile and carrying an elegantly arranged breakfast tray. All the foods I smelled a mere second before were there. A vase holding a rose adorned my tray and next to that lay a scroll tied up with a red velvet ribbon.

"It's beautiful. What's the occasion?" I questioned.

Darla only smiled. She placed the tray on the bed next to me and said, "You should eat. Jake has a busy day planned for the both of you."

Jake, no, oh god! I remembered last night like a bad acid trip. I had been caught spying. I let out another moan, similar to the one of last night.

"Are you O.K.?" Darla seemed genuinely concerned.

"Yes. Urn...can I ask you a question, Darla?"
She shook her head no. "Eat. Jake will answer your questions. Read the scroll. I must go now." And with that she was gone, like a phantom child.

I turned to the tray that only moments before had looked so appetizing. Now, I had a foreboding feeling when I looked at it. I picked up the scrolled note and untied the ribbon. In small neat handwriting the following was written: "Pack a bag and be downstairs in twenty minutes. You'll find everything you need in the closet in your room."

I set the tray off to the side and ran to the closet. Sure enough, there were clothes hanging and shoes on the floor. All were in my size. There was a bag too. They must have sneaked into the room last night and put all these clothes in here. And they must have really wanted me to leave, but yet they are so kind. They laid their lives on the line to help me and I betrayed them. How could I have been so stupid? I paced around the room for what felt like an eternity. I kept nervously glancing over at the clock. Darla had brought my breakfast to me precisely seventeen minutes ago. I hastily flung some clothes into the bag and put on some shoes. The time had come. Not only was I about to lose some great friends, but I would also lose the chance to seek the ultimate revenge on Michelle. I had one minute to get downstairs. I walked over to the door and with a deep breath I made my way down the hall toward Jake.

10

Jake was sitting at the kitchen table with his back to me. "You are right on time, "and he pointed at a chair, facing opposite him.

I moved quiet as a mouse to the chair and sat looking down at my hands in my lap. I could feel his gaze on me. I could hear water dripping from the faucet it was so quiet.

"Do you feel O.K.?" he asked.

"Not really. Upset stomach or something, " I muttered. I still wasn't looking at him.

"Well, that's too bad. I have big plans for today. We could cancel them, but first, do you have any idea what I have planned?"

I could feel his eyes glaring at me. I shook my head yes and still didn't look at him.

"You do?" His question was that in an incredulous voice. "You must've overheard my conversation with Sam. We discussed this in great detail last night. I really wanted it to be a surprise." He sounded genuinely astonished that I knew what had gone on last night. Now, why would he do that if he'd seen me spying? "Oh well...never mind that. Are you packed and ready? We are leaving in 5 minutes."

I felt as if my world was crashing, no, thundering down around me, as if I were a piece of shit, and everything that was happening was something I deserved. I was doing my best not to surrender to the tears welling up inside of me. As I stood to go I sneaked a peek at Jake. His eyes were twinkling. I couldn't believe it. He was throwing me out and he looked like this? Well, I didn't care about him anymore. How could he be like this? How could he look so incredibly happy? I tore my gaze from his, the shame inside me fighting to get out. I muttered something about having to puke and ran upstairs to my room. I wasn't really going to throw up, at least, not until it happened.

As I stood there clutching the porcelain god, I heard a tap at the door. I didn't say anything; I just waited for my hell to start once again. The door swung open and Jake was kneeling down next to me. I shot him a look of utter despair. How could I have misread him? Was I really all that horrible at judging characters? Wait...yes, I was. That's what got me into this mess in the first place. Bowheads and Michelle in the woods. Yes, my character-sniffing abilities were out of whack. Jake had his hand on my back. He was reaching for a washrag, when I got up from my post at the toilet and I left the room. I just wanted to leave. I was making myself so sick. I just wanted to be ousted. I walked over to the bed and grabbed the bag. Before I could leave, though, Jake was holding me by the shoulders.

"I think we should postpone this for awhile. Obviously you aren't feeling up to it. I'm sorry. I thought we could get her today."

I turned to face him. What did he mean by "get her today"? Apparently the confusion showed on my face for he said, "Michelle. We were going bitch hunting. I thought you said you knew?"

He looked as confused as I felt. And this is when my dam broke and my tears splashed down my cheeks. I threw my arms about his neck and wailed. I told him I was sorry for spying. I didn't mean it. I asked, no, begged him to forgive me. I told him I was sick because I thought he was throwing me out. I clung to him like that for a long time.

He said nothing, just ran his fingers through my hair. Finally he spoke. "We wouldn't throw you out, Dee! We might give you a lashing or two, but we wouldn't throw you out!"

He said everyone loved me. Nobody wanted me to leave. Eventually they were going to tell me of their nocturnal habits, but for now, adjusting to people who loved me was a big enough job. He hugged me tight and in an even bigger attempt to mollify me he kissed me on the tip of my nose. I smiled a tentative smile and apologized once again. He wiped a tear from my cheek and pulled me out the door, hollering something about a rendezvous in the woods.

11

We'd been driving for what felt like hours. Sometimes we sat in silence as the scenery rolled by and other times we chatted or sang along with the Violent Femmes tape that was in the cassette player. My mood had greatly improved, and although I had many questions, I knew I would now have the time to hear the answers. Jake didn't explain his activities on the beach last night and I knew better then to ask. I knew when the time came for me to be educated on the subject then it would be soon enough. Until then, I bit my tongue and asked no more questions of Jake.

We were driving to a wooded area on the map. My flesh crawled with goose bumps as I studied this. Supposedly this is the where Michelle lived. Our plan was to camp out for a day or two and scope out our surroundings. We were going to pay Michelle a quiet little visit and then go on our merry way. Jake turned off on a small obscure dirt road that was bumpy and curvy. It was about a mile from Michelle's cabin. Sam was going to meet us there in the morning and then we were going to attack her.

We were silent on the drive down the bumpy road. There was a lot of unneeded tension arising. After we found a clearing Jake turned off the car and let out a big sigh. I turned toward him and simply waited for him to speak. After a moment, he turned toward me and said, "I hope you know without a doubt that we are here for you. There's no backing out on our part."

I tried to hush him, but he would have no part in that. He brushed my hand away from his lips and said, "We all belong together. You, Smiley, me, Darla and Sam. We've all had our share of bad times with the law and with people in our lives and all of us work together to ensure the safety and well-being of each other." He paused to catch his breath and this time I did not interrupt. He continued, "Those people you saw…the ones on the beach with me last night, those are our friends too. You will probably never meet them, but you see how strong we are in numbers. Please, Dee, it's important to me that you know how much I care."

He lifted the sleeve of his shirt and showed me the inside of his left wrist. There was a bar code tattooed on his arm and several numbers were underneath it. His intention was not to shock me with this detail of his life but to show me how seriously he took this so-called "family" he was in. I was shocked, however, but not for the reasons he thought I was. I had sat around many times and drawn bar codes on various parts of my body. To me, it was a symbol that we as humans were all products of the government, guinea pigs, if you will, and I was shocked because someone else had that same idea.

Jake spoke with anger in his voice. 'There has been testing on small children. The government has been implanting them with tracking devices and such and being the outraged individual that I am I got bar coded so the government could blatantly see my anger. I think they shouldn't be so sneaky.

They should have the fucking courage to show what harm they are doing. So this was my little 'fuck you' to the government."

He looked away, almost as if his anger had caused him great embarrassment. I had stumbled upon some wonderful people. I looked at Jake with absolute amazement and a tear escaped. Now it was his turn to look confused.

"Why are you crying. Dee?" He leaned toward me and placed one arm around my neck, pulling me close to him. "Did I say something that offended you?"

I looked at him with adoration in my eyes and said, "You are truly wonderful. I think you are so fucking cool and I think I love you."

I looked down at my lap, waiting for his laugh of rejection, but instead he took my chin and lifted my face and planted a tiny warm kiss on my mouth. He said he never would have shown me the bar code unless he wanted me to be a part of his "family" and then he said be loved me too. He said we would be bonded for life if I would get the symbol on my wrist too and I said I would. He said everyone in the family had one. And then he smiled at me. And then he jumped out of the car and ran around to the trunk and dug around, throwing things out on the ground. Sometimes he had this goofy air about him, one that suggested lunacy of some sort, but the sort of lunacy I knew I could love and trust.

He reappeared in a few moments and he was carrying a tackle box. I asked him if we were going fishing and he laughed. He pulled out a tattoo gun and some ink and he asked me if I was ready to have my bar code "implanted." He plugged an adapter into the cigarette lighter of the car and tested it to make sure it was working properly. I couldn't think of any better time to bond with him and the others so I rolled up my sleeve and awaited the needle.

As he began hammering the ink into my skin I pondered aloud, a question I'd had for a while. Jake listened attentively as I asked, "What exactly is it that you do out there on the beach late at night?"

My curiosity could wait no more. My mind needed to be filled with facts, not speculations. He stopped the machine to add more ink to the needle. I waited for a short time and when he started the needle up without a word I whispered, "Please."

He continued stopping every 25 seconds or so to reload the ink and finally he spoke. "We are a select group of people. We abhor the system that doesn't permit wrongdoers' punishments. We rid the world of trash and undesirables." He was drilling on me when he said this and upon pausing he looked me dead on and said, "We are human garbage collectors." He shrugged and then continued the tattoo. "We find out as much information on our rightly named enemies as we possibly can and then we hunt them down and serve justice." He dipped the needle. "Sometimes the people we stalk have personally done one of us harm, Michelle's dad for example. I'm not sure why he killed Darla's father, but he's a pig and he deserves to die. And then he harmed you. Now he deserves to die a harsher death than before!"

He set the tattoo gun down on his lap and stared intently at his hands. The skin on my wrist was stinging as if I'd been stung by a hundred wasps. I pressed my wrist against my pant leg and then I cleared my throat, forcing myself to ask a question. "What exactly is it that you chant when you dispose of your garbage?" I leaned forward waiting for his reply.

"O.K., it's like this...we catch them, chop them up, burn them and say 'goodnight, yesterday, tomorrow, today and see you later because for all of our lives they will be with us. We're all going to hell. Only, they'll have been there a lot longer then us.'" He shrugged, and then continued. "We burn them as a wonderful prelude for their damned souls. And we speak to them in an old German-French language."

He stopped dead on and stared at me, daring me to ask more questions. Instead, I laughed. Then Jake laughed. He let out a whooping, braying, raucous sound that generally comes out of one's mouth after inhaling five bowls of weed. It came from deep within and mixed with the gravel in his throat.

"We are the avengers of the weak. We take care of our own."

He grabbed my arm and laid it back on his leg and continued drilling the bar code into my skin. I said nothing until he was finished. After he set the gun down and cleaned off my new symbol he stepped out of the car. I took a long look at this bar code. It meant a lot to me. I think I needed this, this longing for a family, for something to believe in. I grabbed a smoke out of the glove compartment and headed out of the car after Jake.

12

Jake had headed down a small twisty path. I assumed it was to be alone. So, like a typical chick in love, I followed him. I wanted him to know I was there for him. And I didn't want to be away from his side for a minute. He obviously heard me trudging along behind while trying to keep up with his long strides. I was breathing laboriously, due to the cigarette habit I'd picked up. Thinking of smokes...I reached into my pocket and dug around all the Kleenexes for that crumpled cigarette pack I'd picked up at the gas station. I had originally thought it was empty and I was gonna toss it in a trashcan, but then upon closer examination, I'd discovered about five smokes. I pulled one out now and noticed it was all crumpled. The second one I pulled out was bent and stupid looking. So, I pulled out a third and it was a winner. It was slightly bent but it wasn't broken. I lit it and caught up with Jake. He'd stopped long enough for me to light my cigarette. Jake had his arms piled high with small twigs and pieces of wood.

We headed back toward the campsite and I breathed a sigh of relief and told him how glad I was for him. He stopped and

looked at me, puzzlement showing plainly on his features.
I shrugged and said, "I'm glad you weren't in the mood to be alone. You've had a trying day and I'm just glad that you are happy."
I felt gawky and immature when I chanced to peek at him. Here was this perfectly wonderful human ready to stick by me through very thin waters. How could I be so ignorant in front of him?
"I'd hug you, but all these twigs would fall and I'd hate to have to pick them up again!" He winked when he said this and my fears instantly drowned.
I grabbed some of the wood and we headed off back toward the campsite. I started thinking of those marshmallows we'd brought with us. I loved nothing more than roasted marshmallows on a stick. Jake must have been psychic for he licked his lips and made cartoon noises and then he burst out with the word, "*Marshmallows!!!!!*"
I dropped the wood in a circle and pulled the lighter out of my pocket. I turned to get Jake's wood. It was lying on the ground behind me but he was nowhere to be seen. I turned back to my fire. It took a minute to get it started, but once it got going, nothing could top it. I turned to go find Jake and that's when I found him. He was standing behind me with his hands behind his back. I jokingly asked him if he had a flower for me and he smiled shyly and nodded "yes." I held out my hands and he handed me a marshmallow on a stick. A white rose for me.
    That night we put our sleeping bags close together. We were lying on the ground on our backs looking up at the vast night sky. The stars were in abundance and the only thing I could hear besides Jake's steady breathing was the small crackle from the fire. My eyes were beginning to close from the comfort of being close to someone I loved.

But as they closed for what I presumed was the last time, Jake hollered, "Look at that!"

My eyes shot open and I stuttered, "What?"

He was pointing at the sky when he said, "The shooting star. Didn't you see it? Make a wish, Dee!"

I told him I didn't see it, but that I would gladly take my wish. So, I thought long and hard and decided to wish for a future with him. No sooner had I finished wishing then Jake was poking me and asking what my wish had been. I laughed at him and told him I couldn't tell. It was against the rules and if you told then they wouldn't come true. Then I reached up to his mouth with my own and I kissed him. He was shocked.

He stopped and looked me dead on and said, "Mine just came true." Then he kissed me again.

Jake was such an innocent child inside. He was artistic. He loved children. He was sensitive and easy to talk to and he loved me too. I'd never before experienced someone as honest and open and easy to read as Jake. I never wanted to let him go. I took a strand of his hair and wrapped it around my finger. When the hair was tight I kissed him with all of my self. I gave him everything with that kiss.

I stopped and said, "Mine just came true."

We fell asleep holding each other, holding onto dreams that had recently resurfaced, holding onto the closeness and companionship of having a lover, holding on. We slept underneath the sky that was full of shooting stars and wishes waiting to be fulfilled.

13

I awoke to lips on mine, last night's haunting dream instantly vanishing. I opened my eyes and saw Jake.

"Good morning." He kissed me again. "Ready to get out of here and start our life of crime together?"

He kissed me again. My "yes" came out garbled.

"Good I've made you some breakfast. After you're done we can go and find Sam. If I know him the way I think I know him, he'll be right on time. He's not a patient person. Hates to wait, ya know?"

I dragged myself out of the sleeping bag and rubbed my eyes. The sky was bright blue with sunlight and the air was cool. I think this was my second favorite time of the day. The first was sundown, the time when the sky would be blowing the heat of the day far away. I ate my breakfast, eggs and toast, and went to the car for a change of clothes. Jake had been packing the car and when I finished changing we were ready to go.

"We're going to drive another mile or so and be closer to the cabin. That way, if things go wrong, we'll be able to get away a little bit faster."

I was so worried. I mean, here were these great people putting their lives on the line for me. What if something went horribly wrong? How would I ever be able to live with myself? We rode in silence for the short distance. We located Sam and we parked beside him.

"Jake! Dee! About *damn* time!" He put an extra menacing emphasis on "damn" and then he took a puff on his smoke.

"Sam." Jake laughed.

"Hey you, got a smoke for me?"

I reached out my hand to accept what he still hadn't offered me. He grunted in my general direction and handed me one.

Sam looked at both of us and with a wicked smile said, "I'm ready to do some hunting."

He put his hands in his pockets and headed off into the woods. Jake and I followed along silently. We'd agreed not to talk. We didn't want to forewarn Michelle that we were coming. The element of surprise was on our side.

We walked a short ways and Sam stopped. He pointed into the woods at a small cabin. He turned to us and grinned. A sense of dread filled me. This is exactly how it happened last. I came upon the cabin and my horror story truly started. Jake sensed my unease and stopped me. He turned me so I was facing him and his eyes reassured me.

But then Murphy stepped in and I was no longer in front of the cabin. I had been transported to a different place. The wind was blowing gentle whispers on my cheeks and through my hair. I could see a small light flickering about 50 steps in front of me. I saw tall dark figures looming above the light. I could hear the damn chanting voices and there was a low murmur, sort of a prayer, being spoken. As I drew closer, I noticed the light was a candle and the figures were those of Jake, Sam, Smiley and Darla. They were dressed in black cloaks. They were holding hands. As I drew nearer still, I saw they were chanting at a grave. Atop the mound of dirt was a single votive candle that was left to flicker alone in the wind. I stepped even closer. I wanted to know what was going on. The wind picked up speed and the votive candle went out. The figures continued chanting. "Gute nacht...bier, aujord bui demain...Gute nacht...Aufbald..." over and over they chanted. I tried not to let my presence be known. I didn't want to be drawn into this strange ritual until I knew what it was. I was content enough keeping my distant vigil. Someone lit another candle and placed it beside the one that had just expired. It was a bigger candle and it put off more light. I was busy looking around, trying to get a feel for what was going on when I noticed a strange looking pile of something lying on the ground next to the grave. It didn't take me long to figure out what it was. Jake reached down and picked all of it up. It was a pile of clothes. I had a suspicion the clothes belonged to one of the chanting individuals, but then I noticed a badge and it looked similar to those of the stinking police force. I took another look at the grave and then I took another look at the badge. I turned to run, afraid of what else I might see, but Jake grabbed me from behind and held me fast. He was telling in order to be in the "family" I must first prove my worth. I was trying to tell him that I loved him, that I got the bar code for him, that I was worthy, but he clamped a hand over my mouth and the other hand reached up and it pulled the flesh from his face. And this is when I screamed. I screamed so incredibly loud. Jake wasn't Jake. The rapist bloody cop was Jake and the clothes he was now wearing belonged to Jake and he was telling me that Jake was in the ground. Sam was a midget hired from the carnival and Darla was really Michelle. Smiley was there but he wasn't smiling and I noticed that Darla/Michelle had a gun pointed at his temple. This was too fucked up. There wasn't any sense in this. I started fighting. I started kicking. I had to get away from this filthy man and dig Jake out of his grave. I managed to claw my way out of the man's grasp and I fell to the ground and started digging. I felt arms grab me and I was back in reality time. I knew at that moment my life was a bad horror story and this was foreshadowing. I took a deep breath and opted for silence. Jake looked inquisitively at me. I just shook my head and told him I was sorry for screaming and giving us away. He said I didn't scream. He looked concerned. I turned and followed the path that led to the cabin. There was no time to explain and there was no explanation for what had just happened.

14

We found ourselves standing at the door of the cabin. Breathing heavily, we banged on the door, but heard nothing. We went around to the windows but the curtains were down and that made it quite impossible to see anything. We hollered and picked up stones and hurled them at the cabin walls but all to no avail. Even Manson was quiet. Odd, because I, being the intruder at one time, had witnessed Manson in action. Oh well, there was more then one way to beat the demon.

As I was thinking this I heard glass shatter and I ran to the other side of the cabin with Jake. Sam had busted a window. Jake gave a thumb up and dove through the window. I made a silent plea bargain with whatever god ruled my world at the moment. I prayed that Jake would remain safe.

Sam put his hands down close to the window and I placed one foot there and leapt up. I closed my eyes picturing the most perfect of revenges and sailed through the window with the agility of a cow. I landed on the floor and felt hands grabbing at me to help me up. But instead of seeing Jake, I saw cops. The filthy pig that had raped me was there, big shit-eating grin covering his huge fat swine face. Instantly I looked for Jake. He was slumped in the corner.

I hollered out a warning to Sam and that's when the knee connected with my stomach. I went down with a grunt. I was able to see Jake. He had the beginnings of a black eye and his lip was swollen. He had his hands behind his back and I assumed he was handcuffed. Fucking pricks move fast. I heard a laugh, a laugh that I was very familiar with. I looked above me and there she was. She was grinning from ear to ear.

I still couldn't believe our plan had been foiled so quickly. How the fuck did they know we were coming here? Had they seen us walking through the woods? Had someone tipped them off? No, that wasn't very likely. Darla and Smiley were the only other ones who knew of our plans to deal with Michelle. I thrashed around on the floor to getaway from the cop's grasp. He grabbed my arm anyway and twisted it sharply behind my back. He bent down to my level, so he was behind me, and he whispered my rights to me and then he threw me against the wall and slapped a pair of cuffs on me. Then he twisted my arm a little harder until I was forced to drop down to the floor again. I was no stranger to this scene, this whole business of being arrested. I'd written hordes of hot checks during my early roaring twenties and I had gotten caught. The cops were nicer then and now I knew how to play the game. The rules were simple. Keep your mouth shut and kiss their ass. That's how they played.

This time though was different and I was pissed. They had absolutely no reason to beat up Jake, not yet anyway. The rules of this game were different. They were making them up as they went. Fine! If they wanted to play this way, I'd play by my rules. And the only rule I had was *"no mercy!"*

I opened my mouth and screamed, *"You backwoods motherfucker!!"*

Instantly I felt a sharp pain in my right knee. The bastard had kicked me and he shouted, "Shut the fuck up!"

"…Go to hell, you Satan motherfucker…" and the boot of the pig came down on my fingers. Inwardly, I screamed. I cursed. I cried in pain. But, outwardly, I did nothing. I didn't even wince. I wouldn't be any help to Jake or Sam if I was hurt too badly . I shut my eyes and prayed that Sam had made a get away. He had to have gotten away. He was our only hope. I collected my scattered thoughts and then calmly spit on the cop's trousers. He took his knee and shoved it into my face, and in the split second before I blacked out, I saw Jake, his head stooped to his chest, blood slowly oozing from the corner of his mouth, and I heard the cackle of the beast, known as Michelle.

15

When I awoke, I had a gnawing pain in my face. I had a bone-crushing feeling in my fingers and my face felt as if it were split wide open. I vaguely remembered what had happened. I looked around. My surroundings were sparsely decorated. There were two metal beds bolted to the wall. Vinyl mattresses lay on top of those. I was handcuffed to the wall by a metal chain. There was a stainless steel toilet, sink, and water fountain combination on one of the walls. Next to that was a heavy door with a small window. The only other fixture in the room was a glaring fluorescent light that hurt my eyes. The smell of crap was prominent in the air. I was so cold. There were no blankets or heating vents and my shoes were gone. The only protection I had from the cold was the clothes on my back. I realized I was in a jail cell. I wasn't sure where, but I wasn't alone. I could hear people laughing. Lots of clanking noises could also be heard. The noises got louder and I realized someone was coming into my cell. I became upset when I saw who it was. He stepped into the cell and silently mocked me. A big toothy grin spread across his face and I was instantly reminded of the Cheshire cat. Just by staring at me, he mocked me. I laughed.

His smile faded and he took a step toward me, as he said, "Haven't quite had enough, have ya?"

I just looked at him, begging him with my eyes to fuck with me just a wee bit more.

"So, sweetheart, tell me…what precisely were you planning to do to me and my daughter out there in the woods? Did you come to wish me a happy birthday?" He looked pleased with himself.

I kept my face neutral but inside I was cursing myself. Nobody had tipped them off. He was there celebrating his birthday and it was just our dumb luck that we picked today to show up. He was so completely disgusting and I was not about to give him the satisfaction of an answer so I willed myself to remain mute. This was the same asshole who'd battered me and raped me and touched me with his nasty, despicable self. He wasn't in spitting range, though I wish he had been. I waited for him to assault me some more but be spoke instead.

"Well, looks like I've got some patty cake to play with your man, little darling, so I'll leave you to your own miserable thoughts for awhile. But don't worry, I won't be gone for long, and when I get back you and I can finish our business."

He pulled up his trousers and stuck his hand on his gun. He said nothing else as he closed the door behind me. It clanged rather loudly and I heard him chuckle to himself as he walked away. I stayed on that metal bed for an eternity. I thought of every possible escape route I could think of and nothing came to mind. I wondered if Sam had gotten away and I wondered what his chances were of bailing us out of jail without getting himself arrested. The chances were slim—slim to none. So, I cried. It was the only solution to a desperate life scenario. I thought back to my last stint in jail. The holding tank was pink, the pink color of Pepto Bismol. Can you fucking imagine? Concrete pink walls. Nauseating. I wasn't handcuffed to the wall but the whole thing was utterly depressing. The air vents spewed out cold air. The police had taken all my jewelry and my belt and my shoes. I hadn't been wearing socks at the time of my arrest so I was left to run around in this cold concrete cell barefoot. I had on cut-off jeans and a thin long-sleeved shirt. The phone in the cell didn't work so I kept annoying the cops about it over the built-in intercom that went directly to the police desk, directly outside my door. They got so pissed they conveniently forgot me and my one phone call I had a right to. They also forgot to serve me lunch. I had used a whole roll of toilet paper up trying to keep myself warm. I'd wrapped it around my legs and I'd spent an hour and a half tearing off tiny pieces and shoving them in the air vent, hoping it would block the flow of air. I'd learned this little trick from someone who I'd been confined with. She was a large black woman who was in for husband abuse. She didn't talk very well and she reminded me of a huge gorilla, jumping around yet sluggish at the same time. Eventually she got led away by one of the guards and I never saw her again. While the guard was escorting her out, he noticed I had no shoes and he promised to bring me a pair. He returned a while later with a pair of oversized white plastic thongs. Surprisingly, I did indeed feel warmer. Not much, but warmer. The next morning, with a stiff neck and a cramp in my right foot, I was informed that someone had paid my bail. I was being released. I was yanked out of my daydreaming by some more clanking and a key turning in the huge heavy lock of the door.

    I opened my eyes and turned over and braced myself for the worst. I was shivering, so I silently cursed myself for looking so weak. I was trying to keep up my tough broad image in case the asshole returned. Now, here he was and I looked like a wimp. A stupid bowhead girl, not able to defend herself. However, my fears ceased a bit when the doorway revealed a gentle looking cop. He walked over to my bed and uncuffed me and told me to be quiet. He laid a blanket at my feet and with a kind smile he turned and walked to the door. Before shutting me in he whispered, "Don't worry, I'll be back. You and your friend will be out of this hellhole in a few hours. Wait until the crew changes shifts and I'll see what I can do. I've always hated that bastard and his daughter." He smiled and left me to analyze this new developing plot in my rather unpleasant life.

16

I was awake, analyzing this turn of events when once again I heard the key turning in the lock. So much clanking and clattering I didn't think I could stand much more of it. I sat upright in less then a second. I figure I had been lying there since the guard left. The kind guard had returned. He motioned for me to join him at the door. He extended his hand and in a low serious voice, he introduced himself as Void. He told me that Jake was out in the hall and we were not to speak to each other until we'd been given the O.K. and once out of this place he would explain who he was and why he was helping us. He placed a pair of handcuffs on my wrists and told me not to be alarmed. Said it was just for show. He spun me around so we were facing each other and he said, "Walk ahead of me. Don't take it personally if I act a bit gruff" I assured him I wouldn't and we turned and left my tiny concrete temporary residence.

It was so good to see Jake. His head was hanging until I stepped next to him. He managed a small grin and then we averted our eyes from each other and simultaneously glanced at Void. He stepped behind us, each one of his arms occupied with careening us down the hallway to safety. We began walking down the long hallway, brandishing on each lengthy side a myriad of doorways. We were approaching an open door on the left hand side and we were ordered by Void to remain silent. The only noise we could hear was the dull drone of a small television set. As if sensing that someone might be in there, Void spoke up. "Keep your step steady and make no sudden moves. You are being transported to the county jail by order of the chief." He spoke in time. I happened to sneak a peek in the door and noticed two cops that were so busy in their paperwork and donuts they didn't even bother to look up.

We reached the end of the hallway and stepped out the door into a garage. There were several cop cars sitting around and Void opened one of the doors and instructed us to slide inside and remain silent. He then locked and closed the doors to the car and walked around back. I turned to see what he was doing and noticed he was pushing a button on the wall. The garage door slowly began to raise and then Void entered once more into the building.

Jake leaned toward me and said, "See if you can get the lock up. We got to get out of here!"

I sat there and smiled. Apparently Void had not told Jake of the plan. Jake probably thought we were really going to the county jail.

"Dee, what are you waiting for?"

But even as he spoke my name Void was coming back through the door toward the car.

"Damn, that was probably our only chance. What the hell's the matter with you?"

Poor Jake. I wanted so badly to tell him. He'd been beaten up severely and he was scared. But I also had the need to mind Void. If a cop had come out and seen us escaping, we'd probably have been shot. And I knew we had better chances if we obeyed Void. Void opened the car door and slid inside. He looked in the rearview mirror as he spoke to us.

"Jake, the name is Void. I'm helping you out of a fucked-up situation. Just stay where you are until we are out of sight of the hell hole and in time I will explain everything to you."

Jake looked at me with this "is he for real?" question on his face. I nodded my head in a yes motion. We backed out of the garage and proceeded down the street. The building was actually rather small. The entire town consisted of nothing more then several houses and a grocery store. I didn't know where we were but I tried not to think about it. It didn't really matter. Void was the one in control now and if he said he was going to explain all in time then I had no doubt that he would. There was something different about him. I could feel it.

We approached the city limit and Void let his guard down a bit. "I'm sorry if I scared you back there, Jake my man. I have to keep my front or else suffer the consequences and there's enough suffering around here without me falling prey too." Jake appeared to be dumbfounded. Void continued, "I've got some pals at county jail who owe me a huge favor. They are already planning your escape from there, which is fortunate, since you're not even going there." He chuckled to himself. I could see Jake tense up again. I smiled to myself.

Void looked in the mirror again and said, "I'm taking you to my vacation home. It's where I go to fish and hunt. No one will even think to look for you there. I won't even be connected with you. As soon as I finish dropping you off I'm going to county to sign your incoming papers and everything will be covered." He continued driving and I noticed we were passing lots of trees and few houses. The scenery was beautiful. Void lowered his voice and I could hear a bit of anger in it as he said, "I've hated

Michelle and her father for a long time. It's just too bad he's my boss. I have a certain duty to him, ya know? But when he does people wrong, I can't stand it. I overheard him telling some of the guys how he got in your pants. Said you liked it and you tried to beat him up when he left you and that's why you were in jail. That guy is a twisted motherfucker and his daughter ain't much better. That's a story for another time however."

We pulled onto a dirt road and drove another mile or two and then turned off into a driveway. The house was set far back from the road. "I hope you two don't mind staying out here. It's only for a little while, until the heat dies down." Void looked apologetic as he said this. I smiled at him in the mirror. I could see that Jake was loosening up.

He leaned forward and said, "Void? I've got a question for you..." He looked uncomfortable. "...Why exactly is it that you are helping us, putting your job and your life on the line for strangers?"

I thought that was a good question. I hadn't thought of it though because we had a pal on the inside. I didn't want to look the proverbial gift horse in the mouth. Void pulled in front of the house and shut off the car. He didn't speak right away; I guess he was bracing himself for what he had to say. As it turned out, it was indeed a horror story. Seemed the whole family was twisted and sick.

"Michelle used to be a big city girl. Her daddy sent her off to college. She got into one of those fancy sororities and thought she was better then anyone else." He turned around to face us. "She never really cared about school. She was more interested in bagging the frat boys and drinking and partying. She used to come into this bar all the time. I was a bartender then and I couldn't stand her. She was a stuck up snob. Once she tried hitting on me. She'd come in and have her gaggle of girly geese following her around."

I interrupted his story with a fit of laughter. I'd always thought it odd that girls had to go to the bathroom in a group and do everything else in a group. They had no independence and basically they didn't feel whole unless their peers surrounded them. I told Void I was sorry for laughing, but he understood. He said he always wondered why girls could never be alone and that's when he started thinking of them as gaggles of girls.

He said, "I refused to go out with her. She got pissed off at me. I used to compare her to a chicken running around pecking in everybody's business. If things wouldn't go her way, she'd get real bitchy and cause a scene. Happened all the time. So when I refused her offer to go out, she decided to do what she does best. She caused a scene. She ordered a drink and then complained that it wasn't made correctly. She threw the glass at me and very nearly hit me in the head." Jake was shaking his head in disbelief, but I thought it sounded just like her. I'd seen her fits of anger. "She's a hellcat. Turns out, she sent another sorority sister into the bar one night. This chick started hitting on me right away and I fell for it, hook, line and sinker. I fell in love with this girl. I think she fell for me too, but Michelle never gave us a chance. She came into the bar one night and had a bunch of flyers. She'd Xeroxed a picture of a wrinkly old man and superimposed my face on that body. Underneath the picture she'd written, 'If you see this man...*run!* He's a wife beater, good for nothing, drunk fool who left me with a child and tons of bills.' I got a bunch of shit for a while from the regular patrons of the bar. No big deal, or so I thought, until she somehow got her father involved and convinced everyone in town that I was exactly what the flyers said. I'm not sure how she did it, and I'm not sure why everyone believed her. Eventually, my boss asked me to take a little vacation until things cooled down. Said it was bad for business or something dumb. I never got my job back. I didn't really care about that, but she ruined my name with all the townspeople and future dates I could have had. Nobody wanted to date me. I eventually left town and ended up here, working for the police department. It was only after I started work here that I realized Michelle's father was my boss. I'd never met him. And he doesn't know about me. I was hoping to somehow seek revenge on her. I know it sounds petty, but I really don't like her because she's spoiled and she ruined a good thing for me. Anyway, you two got arrested and the idea to help you sort of fell in my lap. I figured I could kill a few birds with one big boulder so that's why I'm helping you."

Jake leaned forward and cleared his voice. "If you don't mind me asking…um…well, it seems to me that Michelle did indeed do you an injustice but don't you think you should let bygones be bygones?"

I nodded in agreement. And then I said, "Look, Void, we aren't about to turn down your offer to help us and we appreciate it more than you can probably imagine, but all of this for lost love?"

Void nodded. "The girl I mentioned before, well, we'd been intimate and she got pregnant. She ended up believing Michelle and she left with my son. I've never seen him. And she won't talk to me. I tried to explain to her it was just Michelle's sick twisted mind working to ruin my life but she wouldn't listen. So, you see, there's a lot more at stake here, than just lost love. There's my son. And Michelle will pay."

He closed his eyes and let out a long sigh. I had to agree with him. She was indeed a vicious bitch. Void got out of the front seat and opened the back doors of the car. Jake and I stepped out. Void undid our handcuffs and apologized for leaving them on for so long. Jake and I agreed that it hadn't been a problem.

"I want you to make yourselves at home. Nobody should be coming out this way, so I'm confident you will be safe. I've left some instructions on the table for you and the fridge is stocked. Oh, and I almost forgot, I've arranged for a little surprise."

As he finished this sentence, he pointed toward the back of the house. Mattie was running at full speed toward us. Jake's face had broken out into a full-fledged grin and I leaped toward Void and threw my arms about his neck.

"I don't know how we can possibly repay you for your kindness."

He hugged me back and then he stepped back and said, "No need. Revenge will be ours and that will be my payback. You two go on in and get comfortable. I'll be in touch. But I really need to get to county before I screw everything up." He got into the car and poked his head out of the window. "Sometimes it's good to be a cop. We know everything. I do know that Sam managed to get away and Darla is fine. You should be seeing the both of them very soon. Take care, guys!"

He started the car and drove off. Jake was busy wrestling around with Mattie. He looked so cute rolling around on the ground with his dog. They had a strong bond. I was hoping that Jake and I would bond that way someday. I took a lungful of air and praised Murphy that I was out of jail. Never again. Never did I wish to see another concrete cell.

I walked over to Jake and Mattie and was promptly greeted with a huge slobbery kiss. Then Mattie slobbered on me too and we went inside the house. Jake hit the fridge first. He grabbed two beers out and found a comfortable chair in the living room. I followed him and sat on the floor next to his feet.

"I can't believe the turn our lives have taken." I swallowed this statement down with a swig of my beer.

Jake said he too couldn't quite believe it and he vowed

vengeance on the cop who had beaten him. He picked up the remote control and flicked on the television. A show from my childhood was on the set.

"God, I just love the *Dukes of Hazard*!"

I laughed when I said this and then Jake said, "God, I just love that Daisy Duke!"

I grabbed his knee and gave it a big hard squeeze. He yelped in pretend agony and changed the TV channel. The news was on. We decided to leave it on that channel while the discussion turned to food.

"Void really did leave the fridge stocked. I saw lots of good stuff while I was digging around for a beer. What do you feel like eating?"

I laughed and asked him if he felt like cooking.

"Sure."

He swallowed some more beer. Then he said, "I have an idea. I make a mean spaghetti sauce. How about some pasta?"

I shook my head no. "Michelle ruined pasta for me. She put shrooms in the sauce and then tortured me while I was tripping. Can't eat it anymore."

He put his arms around me and told me how sorry he was. Then he suggested steaks. Again I shook my head no. "Can't stand the way meat tastes."

He said he saw some great looking cheese in the fridge. He suggested grilled cheese sandwiches. I smiled and nodded my approval and gave him the thumbs up sign. He got a skillet out from the cupboard and we set about making the sandwiches. It took all of five minutes and with plates and beer in hand we went to the living room and resumed our seating arrangement. Mattie sat on the floor and looked hungrily at our plates. Jake jumped up and went back to the kitchen. I sipped on my beer while he was gone. I flipped through the TV stations. Nothing much was on. After a few minutes he came back with more sandwiches. He gave me another one, kept one for himself and gave two to Mattie. I laughed at him. He smiled sheepishly and shrugged his shoulders like, "She's hungry too, ya know!"

We didn't talk much. The sandwiches were gone in a few minutes and we just sat and vegged. The news came on and both of us were so tired we couldn't change the channel. It was the same old riff raff of news until we saw ourselves on the screen. It was the same story about the slayings and me and then it made mention of people helping me. "...in custody at this time. Callers are being asked to keep a look out for the third party involved...bald...midget...." We turned the set off and smiled at each other through the growing dimness. Void had made good on his word. They still thought we were in jail. I was feeling a bit slothful, due to inadequate jail accommodations, and I picked up my beer bottle and finished it off.

"I'm going to bed, Jake. Are you coming?"

He nodded and then followed me around the house in search of our bed for the night.

17

The alarm clock was going off. We'd wanted to get an early start on our morning, even though we had nothing to do except sit and wait for word from Void. I reached over and turned off the clock and then rolled toward Jake. He was sleeping peacefully. I started to shut my eyes when I noticed a rank odor emitting from the corner of the room. How odd. I got up to investigate the whereabouts of this smell. I hadn't even taken four steps when I walked right into a wet sticky puddle. It dawned on me what it was as I spied a sight so horrid it made my stomach turn and I puked on the floor. It was the dog. Mattie was lying on her back with her feet stretched out and they were all nailed to the floor. Her head had been severed and placed on top of her belly. In her mouth was a bottle of beer. I tried to think who could've done this and how did they get in the house and how did we not know. The answer pummeled me as quick as I thought the questions. I ran to Jake, a sense of dread filling me, knowing they were still in the house. I shook him. I yelled his name. But he wouldn't wake up. They'd gotten him too! Oh Holy Mary of God! They'd taken Jake from me. I heard my name being called. I looked at Jake but he was peaceful. I looked wildly around the room. I started to puke again and heard the same voice calling my name. They were taunting me, begging me to come see them. I looked at Mattie again. Her belly was split open like a cadaver ready for an autopsy. Her intestines were all over the floor. They were wrapped around her head like worms in the earth. I made a sudden move as if deciding here and now I would kill them all. I would skin off their faces and shit on them. With a sudden burst of energy, I made a mad dash toward the door. Suddenly someone grabbed me from behind. I tried to break free.

"Let go of me, " I snarled. I tried to kick them.

They were laughing at me and saying my name. I tried biting them. They were holding me in an awkward position.

"I said, let go of me!" I was released and turned to look at my captor. It was Jake. He had the goofiest grin on his face. But. But… Jake was dead. I looked toward the bed and he wasn't there.

"Going for some more beer I presume?" he said this while he was still grinning. Beer? Mattie? Voices? I looked on the floor and Mattie was indeed lying there but she was not nailed to the floor and she did not have her entrails hanging out of her body. She had her head on her paws and her tail was wagging slightly. No worms. No bad people. No need to worry. I turned my attention back to Jake.

"What happened to you? You're still alive. The dog's not dead, Jake?"

He had the oddest look on his face, like he'd just woken up in a horror movie, a bad B-rated horror movie is more like it.

He dropped his hold on me and said, "Well, we were sleeping and you woke me up with all the thrashing you were doing. I watched you for while and you got up like you were going somewhere in a hurry. I'm sorry I grabbed you, even though it appears you were sleepwalking. What's wrong? Why did you think Mattie and I were dead?"

I went back to the bed and sat down and said, "I thought you had both been killed. It was awful. It was a warning that I was next. My death would be much worse than yours or Mattie's. It was her, Jake, Michelle and her dad. They were here. I swear it!!"

Jake came over to the bed and put his arms around me and said everything was going to be just fine, stood up and turned so Jake could see the horror in my eyes.

"I don't think everything is going to be fine, Jake. This was way too real—too intense." I told him what I had dreamt.

He shook his head and said he could see why I was so upset but he told me that I could plainly see that he and Mattie were just fine. He pushed me down onto the bed and pulled the covers tighter about me.

"I'm going to kill her, Jake. I know I keep saying this and I honestly mean it. I'm going to kill her." Jake nodded and held me tighter. I tried to sleep. I tried to get the revolting visions out of my head. Nothing was right.

18

When morning arrived, the sun was shining in the window and everything was as it should be. Jake was by my side and the pup was on the floor. I let out a huge sigh of relief. I was starting to believe all these nightmares I was having and I didn't like the sleeping part of my life. I was glad to be awake and know that I was awake. I looked over at Jake's sleeping figure and smiled. He made me so happy. How could I possibly deserve this? The question played over and over in my mind. I had just sat up when the phone rang. How odd. Who would be calling us? Should I answer it? I decided to take a chance and settle my curiosity at the same time and I headed for the phone that was in the kitchen. Mattie jumped up and followed me. I reached the phone on the fifth ring.

"Hello?"

"Hey, it's me, Void!" I sighed with relief. Mattie was whining at the door so I let her out.

"Void, so good to hear your voice. What's up?" I reached into the fridge and pulled out some chocolate milk and a package of cinnamon rolls.

"Well, all is going as planned. I'm coming to get you today. Sam and Darla are waiting for you in the woods and we are all going there to plan a surprise attack."

I took a gulp of milk and then said, "Surprise attack?"

"Yup, on Michelle in the woods. I've arranged for everything and I guarantee that her and her father think you are in the county jail. Trust me, Dee, everything will be fine."

I finished off my milk just as Jake appeared in the doorway. He was yawning and stretching and then asked me who was on the phone. I told him and he held out his hand for the receiver.

"Void, I do trust you. Here's Jake. He wants to talk to you."

I handed the phone to Jake and shoved part of the roll in my mouth. Jake was searching through the fridge too and talking at the same time. I took this chance to slip outside and see more of our surroundings. I also wanted to keep an eye on Mattie. The sun was doing a fine job of warming up the day. The birds in the trees were singing and Mattie was busy looking around for squirrels to chase. I whistled for her to come over to where I was standing and she obeyed me. The land around the house was beautiful. Rolling hills and a few cows and horses dotted the landscape. I stretched and decided to go back inside and see what Jake and Void were up to. Jake was standing at the sink with the biggest grin on his face. Standing with his arms folded and his teeth exposed, he told me that things were in motion and Void would be in the neighborhood in approximately an hour. Just enough time for us to shower and clean up our mess and wait. I went to him and planted my arms about his neck and kissed him on his cheek. There wasn't a need for words. We knew what was coming and we knew what we were going to do. All we could do was wait.

19

Sam was the first person we saw as we pulled up into the clearing. Jake and Mattie were out of the car before it even stopped. I had a bad feeling about this place. It was the same clearing we had camped in previous to being caught. When I tried to bring this matter up with Void and Jake they both waved me aside and told me not to worry. Sam gave a wave and put his hand in his pocket and grabbed a cigarette. He lit it and then came over to me and gave me a hug. Darla stepped out and we all hugged her and told her how good it was to see her again. She told us that Smiley sent his luck. Cheers and laughter were in abundance for we were having a family reunion. Shortly, the unspoken agreement we all wished to participate in would be taking place. We knew where Michelle was and she thought we were in jail, so there was no way this could screw up. I turned to Void to express my thanks and he was staring at me. It shocked me so I couldn't speak. He laughed and said there was no need to thank him. He wasn't just doing this for us. He had a hand in it because he too hated Michelle. Apparently Void had been staying at the house with Sam and Darla and Smiley.

He had called in sick to work and he was there to protect them and also introduce himself to them. They appeared to be getting along nicely enough. Jake cleared his throat and began to talk.

"We need to discuss our plan. We need to make sure it is absolutely foolproof. If we get caught this time, there will be no escaping and Michelle will be allowed to roam this earth forever."

All of us would travel together into the woods. We would be armed with guns, thanks to Void, who had taken some from the station. We would surround her cabin on all sides and ambush would be our goal. Michelle would be our prize. As soon as we caught her we were going to torture her and beat the living shit out of her. Then she would be bound and gagged and thrown in the trunk and be taken on a merciless joy ride. Then I was to have my way with her. And then the others would have their way with her. And it didn't matter what we did, the outcome would be the same: *death to Michelle!*

20

There was a terrifying feeling surrounding me. I wanted to shout but the air was too thick. I was having trouble breathing and I saw images of Sam and some others digging in the sand and carrying large black plastic bags from one pile to the other pile. I saw a bag that had something white poking out of it and I wondered if it was the remains of Michelle. Sam took the bones out of the bag and held them up to the light of the moon and then he said something in a language I did not understand. As I watched on in bewilderment he began to dig a hole, and as if burying the dead was a common occurrence in his life, Sam finished his task. The scene switches and I'm in jail. Only this time, I'm shackled to the bed and I cannot move. The clanking noises return and a guard enters to bring me my lunch. He sets down a steaming hot plate of spaghetti and as I lunge to reach it so I can throw it at him, he leaves. Another ironic scene change. The beloved Mattie has been gutted and nailed to the wall. A cruel twist of fate? An ironic bit of foreshadowing? Either way, the dream stays with me for the remainder of the night. I am worried that something drastically wrong will take place and everyone that I love will be harmed. I don't know what else to do so I force myself back into nightmare land.

21

I awoke to the sun on my face and Jake's arm was draped across my chest. Darla was on my other side, still sleeping and Sam was near the car smoking his morning cigarette. Void was nowhere to be seen. I untwined myself from Jake and hopped up off the ground and made my way toward Sam. Mattie was at his feet, eating her breakfast and she wagged her tail as I approached.

"Good morning. Spare a smoke for a friend?" He obliged me. "Where is Void?" I asked, trying to make small conversation.

"He had to pee. He should be back pronto though. Then I'm gonna wake up the kids and we can start our day. I got things to do, ya know? I don't have all the time in the world to chase bad girls around." He laughed in accordance with his own joke. I had to laugh too.

"Hey, what's every one laughing about? Did I not find a good enough place to use the bathroom? Could you see my butt?" Void came crashing out of the woods, looking confused. This made us laugh even harder and it took awhile before he could understand why we were laughing in the first place.

All of our laughing woke up Jake and Darla. It was nice to have a family, one that loved you no matter what, one that never doubted you, one that could laugh with you. This was my family. I would do anything for this select group of people. They had never badmouthed me and they were on my side one hundred percent.

Now that everyone was awake, it was time. We packed our stuff in the car and silently began the walk toward the cabin. Jake and I had spoken quietly last night about exposing Darla to what lay ahead. I thought she should wait by the car. Jake agreed. Then Darla had spoken. "I know what happened to my father. I know it wasn't a mistake. He wasn't a druggie and I refuse to sit by the car and watch the killer and the evil spawn harm you." She had begun to cry and without a second thought we both put our arms around her and said she could come, but that if anything did happen to us she was to run straight to the car and wait. We didn't want to see her hurt.

So, Darla was a little ways ahead of me and this thought was going through my mind. I wondered what possible motive the fucking pig had come up with to butcher Darla's father. I couldn't think of a single reason. As I continued watching this precious child walk ahead of me I realized just how alone she had been in this huge harsh world. I vowed to protect her, no matter what the cost. I decided if I ever had a child I wanted her to be just like Darla. I could hear Jake behind me as he was softly whistling for Mattie. We hadn't seen her since breakfast. At least she was quiet and didn't bark. I was a bit worried about the dog at the cabin. I had suggested to the others that I should be the first to approach since Manson knew me. Maybe that would prevent him from barking and alerting Michelle that someone was near. Everyone had agreed. As we crept closer, I would move to the front of the line. I turned to give Jake a smile and he had a worried look on his face.

He said, "I can't seem to find Mattie." He was looking around and I told him not to worry. I said it was probably for the best. We didn't want anything to happen to her and this way she was at least out of trouble. He agreed, but still seemed at unease. I gave him a quick kiss on the cheek and then ran up to Darla and kissed her on the cheek and then ran by Sam and planted a kiss on the top of his baldhead. I gave Void a kiss on the cheek and then assumed my position in the front of the line. Nobody spoke. Everyone knew that the time was now.

The cabin had a haunting effect on me. This was the third time I had seen it from the same perspective. Well, that can't be entirely true. The first time I viewed it, it seemed welcoming. The second time, it appeared evil, and this third and final time, I saw it as the killing grounds. I turned around once more and got nods from Jake and Sam and Void and Darla. Everyone was ready. I could put it off no more. In fact, I was ready for the revenge. I crept slowly toward the cabin. No sign of Manson or Michelle. I took this as a good thing. I continued creeping closer and closer until I was next to the wall of the cabin. So far, so good. The others approached cautiously, and when they reached my side, we knew things would work in our favor. With a mighty roar, Jake lunged toward the front door and busted it down. Void followed and then Sam entered. I was next and Darla followed me. The scene was unexpected. It was no surprise we hadn't heard from Mattie. Michelle had been causing problems again. She'd discovered the dog and lured her into the cabin. Oh God damn this fucking bitch. The cruelty. The dog was spread eagle against one wall. It had nails in each paw. It was gutted like in my dream. Its entrails decorated the cabin walls. Before I knew what I was doing, I shot the whore in the stomach. I'd intended to put a bullet in her head, but I had missed. It worked out though, because she was in pain. And I wanted her to suffer for killing Mattie. She knew we were coming after her, but we did indeed take her by surprise. She wasn't expecting us just yet.

Jake was in absolute shock. He was slumped against the wall. I thought he was dead. He looked like a zombie. I didn't know where to focus my energies. Jake or her. She was leaning against one wall with a devilish grin on her face. One hand was clutching her wound and the other was grappling in a desk drawer for something. That something, I assumed, was a gun. I took careful aim and shot at her hand. I missed but she jumped to the side. "Honey, maybe you should let loser over there take aim. He's pretty good with a gun." She pointed in Void's direction. I looked at him and he looked as if he'd just been slapped. I thought he was going to finish her off once and for all and I could tell he was struggling with himself to gain his composure. Michelle wasn't about to give up though. She turned to Jake and said, "Like what I did with your dog?" She laughed out loud, a twisted macabre laugh.

"Shut up Michelle!" I screamed. "You are one demented bitch. Your parents should have had you aborted. You don't deserve to be here." I was shaking from limb to limb when I yelled this at her. Jake was struggling to his feet. He averted his eyes from the remains of Mattie and focused all of his raw anger on Michelle. In one fantastic lunge he slammed his body into Michelle and she grunted and fell to the floor. He began pummeling her face with his fists and he was cussing under his breath. I was happy to see that he had regained his composure. The shock of Mattie was still sending seismic waves throughout my body.

Sam and Darla, meanwhile, had started the process of

removing the dog's body from the wall. Darla was gagging in the severest of ways but they managed to get the dog down and out the door. I turned back to Jake and quietly said, "Slow down, Jake. I want my turn too and Void deserves the chance to beat her."

He slowed and then stopped his sabotage against the bitch. Her head was hanging and resting upon her chest. She was badly bruised by this point. A few spaces in her mouth indicated missing teeth and her wound was still seeping blood.

Good, I thought to myself, *she deserves every bit of what she is getting.*

"I called my father when I finished the dog. He's bringing the entire police force out here. You'll never get away. NEVER!!!"

"That may very well be the case but by the end of the day you will be dead," Void said. "I want you to suffer for the way you treat people, for the way you butchered Mattie, for the way you stole my child from me." He was obviously distraught for Jake and his own personal hell that Michelle had concocted.

She cackled in an attempt to show us she wasn't afraid. She was counting on her dear rapist pig of a father to save her. Void fired off a shot and it hit her in the knee. Her kneecap exploded and blood flew everywhere. She shut her eyes and winced in pain, and then she managed one more smile.

I turned to Jake and Void and said, "We have to go now. If she's telling the truth about her dad we'll all be in trouble soon."

Jake nodded in understanding and began looking for a rope. I mentioned the shed outside the cabin and he stumbled out the door. Void and I spoke not a word. This was a personal moment we were sharing and there wasn't need for conversation. Sam poked his head in the door and said he and Darla would be waiting at the car. I waved and he disappeared. When Jake returned with rope in hand, we started the process of tying Michelle up. It was an awful mess. She was bleeding from various places on her body, and although she didn't put up too tough of a fight, her bleeding knee made things difficult. Since the kneecap had been blown to bits by Void, the remainder of her leg was left to bang against us. I suggested we cut it off, but Jake reminded me of what was to come and how we needed all other body parts for the ritual. Fifteen minutes later she was bound and gagged and we headed for the car.

22

As we came out of the woods the first thing I noticed was the sound of cars—cars, not our car. Everyone seemed to notice it at the same time so we quickened our pace and arrived at our car. I looked down the road and spied chrome. Michelle had apparently been telling the truth. Her daddy was on his way.

"Sam, Jake, look." I pointed. Nodding in unison, Darla was instructed to start the car and pop the trunk. Void stood guard and Sam and Jake and I struggled with the weight of Michelle. We finally managed to get her in the trunk and as we shut the door a shot was fired.

I screamed. Void fired off a shot as the cars drew closer still. He hit the windshield of the first car and it swerved and hit a tree. Void yelled for us to jump in the car and go. We all piled in and Void drove like mad out of the woods. Jake and Darla and I were in the backseat. Jake turned to look out the window and noticed the second cop car had managed to get around the first one and it was now heavily in pursuit. Jake leaned out the window and fired off all six shots. He let out a whoop and yelled, "I got the sons of bitches, shot out a tire, but I can make out another car farther back. Step on it, Void!"

He rejoined us inside the car looking a bit more alive than he should have been considering all he'd been through in the last hour or so. We knew the danger wasn't over yet. The rest of the pig squad would soon be on our tails and we still had some unfinished business to attend to. Jake said the others would be waiting for us at an abandoned lifeguard station where all the enemies were taken and disposed of.

Twenty minutes later we reached it and Void and Sam hauled Michelle out of the trunk and into the station. Jake pulled me aside and said, "I'm sorry I can't give you more time, but you have ten minutes with her. Make the most of it." I nodded and proceeded up the walk to the station. As I entered the boarded up building I heard a few unjustified moans.

"Well, well, well," I drawled in her father's fake southern accent, "what have we here? Why don't you just sit back, get nice and comfortable and be happy that dear old daddy doesn't have to see you exit the universe in such an unpleasant manner." She tried to let out a holler for help but the gag in her mouth wouldn't allow it. I pulled a pocketknife out of my jeans and without a second thought I began sawing her fingers off one by one. It was indeed a bloody mess, but that really didn't bother me anymore. I was smeared with her blood in the cabin when Void shot her kneecap into a million pieces. She moaned and wiggled around but the rope held her securely in place. After cutting off three consecutive fingers I grew bored with my task so I gouged out one of her eyeballs. It hung from the stem and rested on her cheek, staring at me, unblinking. I laughed and wondered out loud if that eye could still see me. I slit her throat the tiniest bit, enough to hurt yet still keep her alive for the following ritual. After slitting her throat, I tried choking her and her blood seeped through my fingers. I reached up and wiped it all over her face and then all over the walls.

"I hope you die a more horrible death than the dog you killed. I hope this shit hurts."

She moaned, but this time it was a moan emitted right before a person passes out. A knock on the door and I ran out, all the way down to the ocean. I jumped in and washed myself off in the chilly salt water. I looked toward the lifeguard stand and saw Void and Jake dragging Michelle toward the campfire that had been built. Approximately seven figures were dressed in black and they were gathered around the fire. I could hear chanting. Michelle was brought to the edge of the fire and Jake spread his arms to the sky.

This was Jake's moment. She had killed Mattie; therefore Jake should be the one to kill her. Sam handed Jake a long knife. It glinted off the sun. Jake kneeled down before her and plunged the knife into the bitch and made a slit from her neck to her gut. Seven people in black began going in a clockwise direction around the fire. They were all holding hands and chanting in a language I couldn't decipher. While they were busy doing this, Jake was throwing her insides on the fire. They crackled and popped like bacon fat on a hot griddle. Seagulls were swooping down and flapping about trying to grab pieces of the intestines. Nobody seemed to notice or care. Jake had grabbed Michelle by the head and he'd finally completed the slit across her throat. Sam left the circle and walked to Jake. He was holding out a red velvet sack. Jake dropped the severed head into the sack and then he dropped the knife in the sack and then he walked over to the circle of people and once again he raised his arms to the sky. In a language I once again could not decipher, he chanted and at regular intervals the others would answer.

About this time I began to hear another sound. Mixed in

amongst the waves and all the voices of my family and the popping noises from the fire I heard something that sounded oddly, frighteningly, familiar. In one of those rare human moments when time really does stop I turned my head and saw him. He was running down the beach, with his gun in his hand and in a horrible second lapse of time I heard the bullet being fired from the gun's chamber. I could see it as it made its way to the fire. As I watched, one of the seven fell.

"*Jake...run!!*" I screamed. Void too had been witness to what I'd seen. He scooped Darla up and the two of them and Sam headed for the car. "*Jake....*" my voice faded as he went down on the sand. I began to run screaming "*no*" at the top of my lungs. The bullet had left a red spray of deceit and failure and my world was crumbling. I was running full speed toward Jake when I heard more shots. I saw another member of the original seven fall. I screamed again and my scream echoed. It drowned out all noise of the waves. I could see Void, running from the car, gun drawn. I could see him shooting at the bastard cop. When he finished his round, there was nothing but silence. I turned my head in time to see the filthy rapist hit the ground and remain there in a crumpled fashion. His gun rested a few feet from his recently deceased body. I ran for Jake. But there was nothing left to run toward. Jake was gone. My world was empty.

Epilogue

It had been three months since the passing of Jake. I was sitting in my newly painted gray room at Smiley's beach house. All of us shared the house, all including Sam, Smiley, Darla, Void and myself. I hadn't gone outside since the terrible occurrence. Nobody had pressured me to do much of anything. I listened to Tori Amos and Portisehead every moment of every day. Their voices rose over the murmur in my head.

My nails were long and I needed a manicure. They wore a nasty green color. I pick at a ragged edge and then bite the nail off down to the tip of the finger. I yell "fuck" when I bite too far and find blood at the end of my finger. Absentmindedly I put a cigarette in my mouth. With lethargic eye I find a match. Smoke gets in my eyes so I shut them. But shutting them brings to mind pictures of Jake. I had felt alone since the day of Jake's murder. The one true love I knew was suddenly ripped from me. I searched for the blue nail polish. This wicked green had to go. Blue was more soothing. I close my eyes again and the thoughts of Jake flickered behind my closed lids like a candle flame.

"Can I ask you a question, Dee?" He looked so sweet when he said this.

I nodded my head in a yes motion.

"Could you make me a promise, never to leave me? Is that fair of me to ask?" He looked down shyly, afraid to hear my answer. "I've thought about us for a long time now. I was afraid to be with you. I was afraid you would leave." His head bent down to his chest.

I nodded my head no and kissed him and then my eyes open and I realize all of this had taken place the night before we stalked Michelle. The bitch was dead but she had managed to ruin me.

I close the nail polish and fall to my side in the fetal position. My arms are in the air so my nails can dry. Feelings were all I had now: memories of Jake, Jake touching me, Jake kissing me…Jake. Sad feelings of him were all I had. He was gone. I was sad. I lift my head. I hold it in this position for a few seconds. I let it drop with a thud.. Nothing. Lift head. Hold in position. Thud. Nothing. Nothing. Nothing. I close my eyes and a pattern appears. Handprints in red going across white walls. It would only be a matter of time before the police found me. They had my prints. I had a record. I was wanted for the deaths of sorority girls and Michelle. A loud pitiful moan escaped my lips. It was only a matter of time. My head split into several different characters. They all told me what to do. But I choose not to listen. I let Tori sing me to sleep. And then I dream of my Jake.

CPSIA information can be obtained at www.ICGtesting.com
Printed in the USA
LVOW06s0319240713

344093LV00002B/136/P